The
Wonderful
Life
of
Senator
Boniface
and other
Sorry
Tales

The Wonderful Life of Senator Boniface and other Sorry Tales

ISBN 9789789340767

First Published in Nigeria by:
Bookvine
An imprint of Vine Media Services
12b, Talabi Street, Off Adeniyi Jones, Ikeja
Lagos State, Nigeria.
Tel: +2348038069951, +2348055696965
Email: bookvine@vinemediang.com

Cover design: Derek Murphy
Author photo: DUDU
Interior design: Jera Publishing, Georgia, US

This book is a *Shecrownlita Scribbles* Production

The Wonderful Life of Senator Boniface and other Sorry Tales

AYO SOGUNRO

A BookVine Imprint
A Shecrownlita Scribbles Book

For Yuppy, Mikky and Dessy

A QUICK NOTE

You, probably, paid some honestly earned money to get to read this book. Or, at least, you intend to invest some time and energy in the reading. If, at the end, you believe you haven't received enough value for your investment, my apologies. And, if you really feel strongly about your time and energy, then these are the core people to blame for the existence of the book:

Goke—for failing to stop me when I got the idea;
Afolashade—for energetically pursuing the idea;
Enuma—for always saying I've got the best ideas; and
Toyin—for always having an idea.

And then you have *Kayode Faniyi, Mena Eremutha, Onome Adeyemo, Rosemary Tsetim,* and *Opeyemi Bello*—for either helping me to reshape the ideas, or inspiring me with even more.

And there are the people who have been involved in the production of the book, especially *Chinelo Onwualu, Seun Salami* and, of course, the folks at Vine Media.

You can get your money back from them all. But if you're still not satisfied, I have even more names, set out in a long list, to give you.

CONTENTS

The Death of the Muse

The troubles of our blood and state
The epic battles we draw in boardrooms
The stands against the flaws of fate
The valiant skirmishes of the bedrooms.

With these and more, we sink desperate
Lone stragglers through life's classrooms
Our pens lie wasted on a blank template
We live on, but the Muse lies in state.

PREFACE:
Life, The Universe and This Entire Book

"I always think that the chances of finding out
what really is going on are so absurdly remote
that the only thing to do is to say hang the
sense of it and just keep yourself occupied."

DOUGLAS ADAMS, THE HITCHHIKER'S GUIDE TO THE GALAXY

Don't Panic, Yet

Prefaces are dull and there should be no compulsion for a reader to be subjected to the agony of enduring one of these monstrosities. The preface of this book is no exception to the general rule—and even more compliant with the opening aphorism is this introductory preface, disguised as a paragraphed introduction. This preface would probably not add any value to the enjoyment of the book; neither will it reveal some extraneous insight. Therefore, if you are solely inclined towards the entertainment value of the book—which you rightfully should be inclined to—you can stop right here and pursue your reading pleasure.

On the assumption that the previous paragraph did not dissuade you from the futility of a scholastic approach to this book, here's another excuse why you should skip this section. On some other day, when you are suffused with the requisite measure of patience and the proper disposition required to tolerate a convoluted dissertation, you can open up this page again and fill a few minutes of the day with some epistemological quandaries. This is more sensible as the preface is, hopefully, not going to fade from the pages of the book. So go on, enjoy the book and ignore the pontification.

However, if you intend to pursue a pedantic course with the fastidiousness of a studious character (preferring to read fiction like an academic treatise and not like a captured dream), or if you have suddenly developed an odd fascination for the mysterious contents of this preface—then stay awhile, and we may yet answer the questions you're eager to ask.

Because These Are Mostly Harmless

The stories in this book are written for entertainment—any other ramification is fortuitous. If you can derive an evening's pleasure from any of these stories, then my primary purpose for writing these would have been achieved. Of course, this does not preclude the existence of hidden meanings, symbolisms and staggered interpretation. But riddles should be diversions: tidbits provided for the metaphysically inclined and the literature student, the esotericism of Strauss notwithstanding. In any case, interpretations are rarely facts, and when it comes to hidden meanings, Oceania has always been at war with Eastasia.

Of course, the defocus on symbols does not exclude my intention to create scenarios that shift away from the first-world's view of African literature—that kaleidoscope of yearning Africans, buffeted by the (imagined) circumstances of the gory jungle, trampled under the dust of "the single story", seeking nondescript redemption from the West—and showcase, instead, the strong individual humans, not just "Africans", changing their fortunes and rising against the (imagined) circumstances of the gory jungle, but without any help from the West. In simpler words: the African character in a story is equally able to redefine his destiny without necessarily having an American visa in his pocket.

But look for the story first, the harmless, unassuming story. The important goal in any piece of fiction is the ability to tell a story. Art should not be confused with social science, and neither should a story be mistaken for a lecture.

Except That Intrusive "Vogon Poetry"

Poetry, like all formless characters, should be viewed with suspicion. However, here is a brief defense for the inclusion of poetry in what is essentially, a collection of prose tales. The core value of any piece of poetry is its ability to capture the imagination with the subtlest of expressions. Poetry's allure is in its nifty and thrifty use of language. Prose is more generous in quantity: a writer has more freedom than a poet in the number of words he or she is allowed to portray a scenario.

And so we have both the narrative capacities of prose and the illuminative influence of poetry. This symbiosis translates, hopefully, into higher value for you, Dear Reader. Therefore, while each story can be read superficially, the poems lend that little bit of subtlety that transposes the prose from the elemental narrative into a compound metaphor. In proper English: each poem is intended to make its corresponding story even more enjoyable.

Now, an astute reader may point out the seeming contradiction between a harmless piece of prose (as we have tried to argue above) and lines of poetry potentially subversive in interpretation. With such a connection in place, the didactic significance becomes inescapable and the story becomes more than just a story. This is a fair observation. One should, however, not confuse the incontinent interpretation of poetry with the plot-defined significance of verse — as presented in this volume. Standing by itself or in an anthology, each poem is subject to a variety of meaning, to be chewed over by critics of the genre; but when sharing explanatory space with prose, the verse becomes less fickle and should be treated as such.

But That's Somebody Else's Problem

Naturally, the separation of entertainment from symbolic interpretation does not imply that the stories here offer no social concern or criticism. Literature can rarely be separated from life—and even then, only mostly in the form of highly abstracted art. These stories are anything but abstract; life is grounded in a continuous stream of sorry tales—as well as uplifting ones. And on a social scale, the Nigerian socio-political landscape is host to a number of issues that allows for focused concern.

Take our entrenched spirituality, for example; our moral and religious systems have encouraged the false idea that a good spiritual life is inevitably rewarded with riches. And so we have made heroes out of the Bishop Okikiolas traversing the social landscape—ready to administer an overdose of brain-numbing medication—smooth operators in the guise of spiritual caretakers.

Naturally, a nation is defined by its heroes, but we have also managed to subject even these to grave misconceptions. Senator Boniface may have the best intentions, but this does not eliminate the propensity for personal machinations.

This idea is properly illustrated by a recent society-wide fracas surrounding the characters of two illustrious, now deceased gentlemen, Chinua Achebe and Obafemi Awolowo, sometime after the former published his book: *There Was a Country*. The popular tendency for misconception generally masked a logical fact: Achebe was a great writer and Awolowo was a great leader, but it is wrong to assume that the one always wrote accurately or that the other always acted righteously.

But this volume does not set out to solve socio-political complications or find a cure for cancer. No philosophic or political leanings are proposed here to cure economic ills. Read for enjoyment and maybe pick up a lesson or two.

In Case You Are Paranoid

Death is inevitable. A presence we get used to and move past. It becomes trivial because of its generality. Familiarity keeps breeding contempt. Of course, the death of an individual is important to that individual, and to his society—if he inhabits a sane one. However, death as a concept—or if you prefer, a personification—is not special. Its ordinariness is, in fact, amusing.

Here's A Deep Thought

The stories in this volume have not been presented in any particular order of significance, except, maybe, according to their narrative nature. Chaos theory suggests otherwise—but literature is not bound by scientific principles.

This Is Not Entirely Unlike Life

And let's leave it at that, lest this preface emerges as a critique of its own text. You may find that the words in this preface are, ultimately, misleading—but that's, literally, in your hands. And so, Dear Reader, this is the point where you throw up your hands and say: "Hang the sense of it!" and just keep yourself occupied. There is nothing more to be said, and the book is waiting to be read—or reread. Hurry on along.

AYO SOGUNRO
(LAGOS, 2013)

Pavement Pounding Philosophy

Past the parade
Of professional papers
Printed and proper
Precursors and pointers
To the paralysis of a predictable people

Past the parade
Of persuasive participants
With protests and placards
Protected by particulars-privy policemen

Past the parade
Of pink-phizzed prostitutes
Presenting personnel profiles
Of perverse political parties

Past the parade
Of profiteering panjandrums
And pectoral punks
Pursuing the prey
Of pirating politicians

Past the parade
Of pick-pocketing peacemakers
And pregnant proselytes
With pretentious postures
Preaching presidential prerogatives

Past the parade
Of pavement pounding philosophers
—Including me—
Politely preventing
Personal participation

ONE:

A Loss of Confidence

A member of the Senate or of the House of Representatives may be recalled as such a member if: (a) there is presented to the Chairman of the Independent National Electoral Commission a petition in that behalf signed by more than one-half of the persons registered to vote in that member's constituency alleging their loss of confidence in that member; and (b) the petition is thereafter, in a referendum conducted by the Independent National Electoral Commission within ninety days of the date of receipt of the petition, approved by a simple majority of the votes of the persons registered to vote in that member's constituency.

SECTION 69, CONSTITUTION OF THE FEDERAL REPUBLIC OF NIGERIA, 1999.

"It is impossible to vote out a Nigerian minister."
MAJOR KADUNA NZEOGWU

The Honourable Mr. Adekunle Quadri Sodipo, current Representative of the Abeokuta South Federal Constituency and current Speaker of the Nigerian House of Representatives had bitten off more than he could chew.

He therefore had to pause midway through the point he was making, and concentrate instead on masticating the piece of fried chicken in his mouth. This distraction from his feeding annoyed him, for he hated interruptions of any sort—except when *he* was the one making them. The incorrigible chunk of meat he had shoved into his mouth was, however, not as annoying as the little man who sat across the desk from him, clutching a ream of tired-looking A4 paper and mouthing uninformed opinions about the mechanisms of government.

"That is our position, sir," the little man concluded in a small, but firm, voice.

The little man shifted visibly on his seat, uncomfortable in the presence of the Federal Speaker. He tried to be calm, but the Speaker unnerved him. He had made his assertive remark several seconds earlier, but he was unsure whether the Speaker's silence was deliberate or a sign of disinterest. So he repeated his statement, with emphasis on the "sir", and then kept quiet. He looked hungrily at the unfinished plate of vegetable-garnished rice and chicken before the Speaker. But the Speaker chewed on without acknowledging the little man's gaze—if he noticed it at all.

The two men were in the Speaker's country home in Abeokuta. The Speaker was dressed casually, in a collared shirt that stylishly fitted his body frame, while the little man wore a grey suit, clearly too big for him, over a shirt that—stereotypically—was once white, but could now pass for a type of yellow. Beneath the muted comfort of the Speaker's home office, the discreet humming of the air-conditioner and the distant roar of the electricity generator vied for auditory space.

Mr. Kunle Sodipo, who ordinarily resided in Abuja, had arrived in the sleepy town of Abeokuta three days earlier to intervene in an on-going battle slowly consuming his native state's House of Assembly. He was an expert in troubleshooting legislative conflicts; his favourite method of discipline in the Federal House was the unhesitant suspension of members who refused to toe the official line—and the official line was whatever favoured him personally.

With the intervention of the Speaker—he had engineered the suspension of the troublemaking faction—the political dispute in the state's legislature had been settled. Euphoric at another validation of his political skills, he had decided to spend a few more days in his hometown before travelling to Lagos, and then flying back to the political skulduggery of Abuja.

Beyond his political manoeuvrings, he had had even more reason to be in excellent spirits. Earlier in the morning, the Vice President had called him bearing good news. In exchange for the Speaker's continued political support, especially towards the party primaries scheduled for January, the President was offering the Speaker an opportunity to purchase his official residence in Abuja from the government at a highly subsidised commercial rate.

"Subsidised? My *Oga*, explain this better," the Speaker had joked.

"Well, Mr. Speaker, let's say Twenty Million, as a starting price."

The Speaker had sat up at the Vice President's response. "Twenty? I thought the residence was constructed at ₦300 million? Is there a catch here?"

The Vice President had laughed loudly. "That's why we call it highly subsidised, my brother."

"Then God bless subsidies." Both men laughed. "Tell Mr. President he has a deal."

"Excellent, we will discuss this when you are in Abuja—if the President has not auctioned off the city by then, that is."

The two men laughed again over the joke, and the Vice President rang off.

Now, the Speaker reflected; this trip was being soiled by the little man in front of him who had been spurting nonsense for almost an hour. But hometown was where he allowed his mates to rub shoulders with him, and that was why the little man now had this opportunity to visit his home, meet him in person and feel important for a little while.

The Speaker cleared his throat as the last piece of meat finally went down his throat. He was an educated man, and he could deal with situations like the one he faced now in an intelligent manner. As his colleagues in the Federal House could testify, he had a way with words.

"Corruption. That is what you accuse me of," the Speaker began quietly. "Normally, I would laugh you in the face and immediately direct you out of this place, but being the considerate person I am, I will not. In fact, in order to enlighten you and put an end to nonsense of this sort, I will give you a little lesson in practical politics." He sipped deliberately from the glass of water beside him before continuing in an even tone.

"What do you mean by corruption? How do you identify an act as corrupt? Listen, with the type of governmental structure we have in Nigeria, it is impossible for a political leader to be corrupt all by himself. You might as well divide a number by zero! The corruption you see in this government does not stem from the politicians who occupy office; instead, its roots are grounded deep in the heart of the civil service, and in the general society.

"You, think about it and tell me; what does a newly elected President know about the machinery of government? What does the average politician know about economics? What could a President with a university degree in Chemistry contribute to the task of balancing the budget of the federation? Nothing! See, when a man is elected to a position, he comes in with ideas. He has visions! He intends to achieve a lot—and he wants to make a name for himself. So he appoints ministers and assigns them portfolios. The ministers then seek the advice of the heads of service and permanent secretaries in their ministries on how to achieve the directives of the President within the shortest possible time. And what happens next?"

He paused, as though expecting an answer from the little man. The little man said nothing. The Speaker continued, more animatedly.

"The *goddamn* civil servants point the ministers in the wrong direction! They show *us*, instead, how and where to skim. I am an honest man, but I am also a practical one. If myself, or any other politician, refuses to co-operate with these schemes, the civil servants will frustrate their tenure. The President does not award contracts, neither do I. It is the civil servants who pick the contractors. Our job is to co-operate with them while serving out our limited term—and maybe we may even get more time for good behaviour. Listen, the blame for corruption in government rests solely on the civil service at all levels, in all agencies and all parastatals!"

The Speaker's tone had risen, but he was not shouting. He sipped from his glass again and depressed a button fixed to his desk. Almost immediately, the door opened and a tall, stout man dressed in the black uniform of the Nigerian Police Force came into the room. His police orderly gave the impression of a black box with appendages. The service pistol sticking out of the holster on his left hip seemed like a parasitic demon: a tool of conflict, brutal and incongruous against the background of the domestic setting.

"John," the Speaker waved towards the dishes before him, "Call the maids to clear these plates if you can't do it yourself."

"Ye'sir," the policeman said, bowing deferentially before withdrawing from the room.

"But what has everything I have said got to do with your accusations?" The Speaker asked, without showing interest in waiting for an answer. "Nothing. Nothing at all. The important point is that, in spite of your allegations, and in spite of this wretched list which you call a petition, my people love me."

As if to buttress this last point, John came back into the room with two young women in their early twenties. Both women had the dark skin and heavy bosoms typical of the townswomen. They curtsied to the Speaker and started to clear the desk of its culinary occupants. The Speaker kept quiet while they worked, his eyes deliberately following the nubile movement of their bodies. A smile played around his lips as they went out of the room, with John following them.

"You say the people want me out. Where are the riots in the streets?" The Speaker cupped his left palm behind his left ear, and cocked his head in mock attention. "Do you hear any protest? I don't. Why? Because there is none! Those papers with you are only fit for the groundnut sellers. Do you really think you can recall the Speaker of the House of Representatives by waving around the signatures of some jobless polytechnic students? You are hilarious. Do you hear me? You're just hilarious!"

The little man brought out a handkerchief and nervously wiped his brow. He was sweating despite the coolness of the room. This meeting was not going as he had anticipated. He now tried to recollect the session in Lagos three weeks earlier when the President of his NGO had assured him that the Speaker was bound to take him seriously when he saw the petition calling for the Speaker's recall. The little man had been selected to have the first confrontation with the Speaker as he lived close to the Speaker's country home and could monitor the Speaker's movements within the town. The NGO had painstakingly obtained the signatures of nearly all the members of the Speaker's constituency for the petition. If the Speaker refused to behave better, the President of his NGO had concluded, the list would be taken to the electoral commission for further action. *The constitutional provisions were sacrosanct.* That, at least, was certain.

The little man tried that line of argument. "Sir, this is not about the civil service or government in general, this is about you and your constituency. We have lost faith in you. Like I said earlier, we are tired of the allegations of corruption against you and your continued disregard for the welfare of the constituency. We are citing the Constitution, and Section 69 states that..."

"And who do you think writes the damn Constitution—the people?" the Speaker snapped. "We, the leaders, write it! Let me rephrase it more specifically. *I* write it. I dictate every damn line in it, every comma, semicolon and full stop. I know every sentence of your damn Section 69."

The Speaker continued, "And the only reason why your Section 69 is still in the Constitution is because it's damned ineffective." The Speaker considered his own statement, nodded and smiled cheerfully. Then he stared hard at the man before him as he paused for dramatic effect.

"Read Section 69, again. You will never recall a single legislator in Nigeria as long as that clause remains the recall provision," he concluded with a wide grin.

The Speaker yawned and consulted his wristwatch lazily. "Well. Mr.— *er*," he paused. "Sorry, I forget your name. Now, if you have no other issues to mention, would you please show yourself out? I have heard enough from you on this matter. I have given you an hour of my time; surely, that's enough. There are, to invoke that useful cliché, matters of state awaiting my urgent attention." The Speaker stood up.

The little man remained on his seat, in mild shock at the arrogance of the Honourable Kunle Sodipo.

"Mr. Speaker, sir, our petition is signed by over thirty-five thousand people from the Ogun Central constituency. It took us nearly six months to compile this list; signed against the names and addresses of almost the entire electorate—and we validated each signature! Do you think we are unserious about this issue? The people of Abeokuta are fed up with your self-enrichment at their expense!"

The Speaker looked at the little man quizzically. "I thought I told you to show yourself out. Do I need to throw you out myself? Besides, do you really think I can't buy out every person that signed that list? One bag of rice per signature will do the trick! I will get the electoral commission to invalidate the petition even before you submit it for approval. Now, will you get out?"

The Speaker stood up and looked at the little man with a clear implication that the meeting was over.

At this point, the little man received sudden insight into everything that was wrong with the existing political system. *The system was flawed—the natural right of individuals to make decisions by themselves or elect representatives for that purpose had been replaced with the illusion of a ballot box parading as democracy.* It was astounding. All his life, he had fought for democracy—but now he concluded to himself that democracy was an overrated idea. In fact, it was better to have the traditional monarch who would abdicate the throne or commit suicide at the insistent demand of his people than a democratic politician who spends a term in office without regard to the electorate's requests. The important factor was not the system of government that was in place, but the extent to which the rulers paid attention to the needs of the governed.

The constitutional provisions were not sacrosanct.

A wave of emotion coursed through the little man as he felt, resting upon himself, the responsibility of voicing the thoughts and frustrations of the multitude. In a desperate attempt to fully confront the Speaker with his embittered thoughts, the little man dropped the papers on the table and jumped up from his seat. He seized the Speaker by the collar of his shirt, twisting the Speaker forward towards him and, by that singular action, committed both a civil wrong and a criminal offence under the laws of the democracy in which he had now lost faith.

The Speaker was bigger, but he had been caught off-guard by the little man's assault and he stumbled across the desk. He quickly depressed the button on his desk as he fell. The door opened almost immediately and John came in. John cursorily assessed the situation and drew his handgun. The little man did not release his grip on the Speaker's shirt. The Speaker stared at the little man with amused contempt as he struggled back to his feet, then he spoke to the orderly.

"John, take this fool of a thing out of here and lock him up in Eleweran for a month. Tell the DPO that you are acting on my orders."

The little man, his grip still on the Speaker, turned to face the policeman and, with his other hand, pointed angrily at the papers now scattered on the desk. He spoke rapidly in Yoruba, his pitch increasing with every syllable.

"You are an Abeokuta man, are you not? Your father, mother, sister, brother, aunts, cousins, nephews, nieces, friends and the whole of your people want this terrible human being out of an office they elected him to in the first place. They want him to stop the abuse of their good name. They have lost confidence in his ability to speak the truth and defend their rights. This same man whom you defend takes our daughters for his pleasure. He spends our money on himself, and listens to nobody. You know this man, you know how he got here—we thought he was a different sort and voted for him happily, but he is even worse than his predecessors. Look at you. What has he done to improve your life apart from the beggarly spare change he throws your way? You hold the gun and you have the handcuffs. Lock me up. Shoot me, if you want. This day will pass by, and tomorrow you will remain here, an enslaved person, dutifully carrying out the wishes of your oppressor. But, remember, it is people like you that allow people like him to spit on people like us."

The little man spat on the table, released his hold on the Speaker and shrugged at John. The policeman looked at the little man, his gun still pointed at him, and then hesitantly, he swung towards the Speaker and shot him twice in the chest. The Speaker lurched backward, the surprise on his face permanent as he died in his chair. John walked to the desk, picked up some sheets of the blood-stained ream and held them up for the little man to see.

John spoke in English with a heavy Yoruba accent. He measured his words as he faced the little man. "You may think some of us bend backwards too much. But in every curve, there are an unknown number of sharp points. You've seen one of the sharp points today. I have no confidence in him either. You have my signature."

The little man stood shocked, more still than the dead man, and stared at John in terrified silence. John looked bored; his stare was that of a man who had done his part, and nothing more. The humming of the air-conditioner and the roar from the electricity generator occupied the auditory space as the two inconsequential men who had forged the first consequential link in a chain of consequences stared at each other.

They stared at each other for a while, and then they stared at the body of the Honourable Mr. Adekunle Quadri Sodipo, former Representative of the Abeokuta South Federal Constituency and former Speaker of the Nigerian House of Representatives. The politician who had bitten off more than he could chew.

Transferred Aggression

I don't want to hear you talk.
I've had a messy day. Don't add to it.
The pain of a life in urban stress
Sharpens the edge of my rage.
Run down the road, play with friends.

I don't want to hear you nag.
My boss did the same through the day.
Don't come here and start afresh
The sorrows of my servile life.
Go to the kitchen, cook your meals.

I don't want to hear you preach.
What do you know of hell on earth?
My soul already moves from here,
Dreaming of days when I was unborn.
Go next door and sell your wares.

TWO:
The Victory of the Red

"This is Lagos. All kinds of
things happen in this city."

ANONYMOUS

It was a full moon. The madness tore at his brain and the edges of his vision grew blurry. A tinged, blurry vision. As though with blood. *Red.*

Red Devils.

The pain in his head flared anew at that thought. The images from the television screen at the football-viewing centre flashed like a gigantic cinema in his mind. The headache was an unrelenting rush of blood pumping in and out of his cranium. *This is what it means to be mad.*

Eto'o scored a goal. The game had barely even started, and suddenly, a streak from the right, and the dribbled defenders scattered like skittles. And Eto'o scored a goal. *How could that have happened?*

Red.

Devil.

His steps were unsteady as he began to walk home. His toes curled in his leather slippers, a physical manifestation of the throbbing in his head. He shook his head and tried to hurry on. He was anxious to lie down and forget about the defeat of the Red.

Then Messi scored another.

The headache pounded on. It now took the form of a slow throbbing that began at the base of his skull and worked its painful way up towards the back of his eyes, where it became a locomotive chant, knocking against his forehead in sing-song scorn.

Bam-bam, bam-bam, bam-bam.

The amorphous chant in his head began to crystallise into the rhythmic song of a thousand mocking voices: *two-zero, two-zero, two-zero, TWO-ZERO, TWO-ZERO.*

He clenched his fists, painfully. But even as he did so, the pain continued to beat an agonising rhythm in his head. His skull was a box possessed by a wild devil beating on a drum. He constricted his forehead to reduce the throbbing, the lines on his face were like crevices, but he felt relieved.

The Red again.

Somewhere in the dark distance, he heard fading jubilant screams. The Ebute Metta night, which was ordinarily slow of tempo, had exploded into a flurry of activity in the wake of the football match. The conclusion of the European Champions League, in a far-off country, on another continent, had elicited thunderous howls of ecstasy from the fans of victorious team and corresponding depression from those on the losing side.

Two-Zero.

Earlier in the evening, when he left home for the local football-viewing centre, he had felt fine—exhilarated, in fact. He could have watched his team, Manchester United, play the championship final against Barcelona FC from the comfort of his own home, but his father, a football enthusiast who was just as passionate about soccer as he was, was a Barcelona fan. He wanted to enjoy the match without the continuous stream of commentary his father was bound to offer. There were no headaches then, just the anticipation of the forthcoming match. He had left the house with a spring in his step.

His team should have won. By all the laws of logic, they should have won. After all, weren't they the champions of the English Premiership, the only ones to win it three times in a row? They were also the current Champions of Europe. What other team could stop them? What was Barcelona FC? Barca—it even had a stupid nickname. *Barca*—the kind of name one would give a rabid dog.

Secure in this knowledge, the evening had begun with an air of bliss. Until the first ten minutes of the match. Then everything went downhill. And the headache started.

Now as he walked home slowly, taking the shortcuts leading to his house, and avoiding the jubilant horde of Barcelona fans in the main street, the headache pressed harder against his temple. He had no desire to meet anybody. He could not face anyone now, friend or foe. And the thought of the inevitable exchange with his father only made his headache worse. Worst of all, he had on his Manchester United jersey. *His red jersey.* He could not face any taunts now. All he wanted was a bed and a pillow, and an assurance that the headache would subside.

It was not that his club had never suffered defeat before; life was a string of several small defeats and a few major victories. But to have banked all of one's hopes and aspirations on the outcome of one singular event—to bet all of one's earnings on a stake—and lose. That was pain. He felt the tears springing to his eyes.

"Hey! Up Man-U," a teasing voice called from behind him. He looked back; his neighbour's twelve year-old son, also returning from the viewing centre, was behind him. He had no desire to talk to anyone, but he stopped, and allowed the boy catch up with him.

The boy ambled up to him and began his own staccato commentary on the match.

"Bro, did you see the way Eto'o scored that first goal? That was a goal, *men!* I just knew that Man U could not win the match after that first goal. What was wrong with your team anyway? You people think you are always better, *abi*? This is Barca o. You can't mess around with Barca." The boy went on at length as they walked on, and the incessant tirade that poured into his ears soon began to make his headache pound even faster.

Two-zero, two-zero, two-zero, TWO-ZERO, TWO-ZERO.

Unable to bear the pain any longer, he turned to face the boy prating at his side: "Shut up!" And he followed his shrill scream with a swift motion of an upraised hand that found a landing spot on the boy's skin—hitting the boy firmly on the cheek. The boy reeled.

He was surprised by his own action, but the blow he dealt seemed to reduce the headache. And as the boy tried to gather his wits, he moved towards the boy and gave him two more slaps in furious succession. Then he drove a balled fist into the boy's face. He watched the blood spurt out of the boy's nostrils and the image that emerged in his mind was of a football captain uncorking a celebratory bottle of wine.

Let the Red pour, let the Red flow, let the Red come.

With that thought running continuously in his mind, he drove blows into the boy's face, each syllable of the phrase running in his head punctuated by a corresponding assault. He looked down. The boy was still, lifeless. The Red Devil had been appeased. And his headache was gone. For now.

A victory of the Red—at last.

🍺

He hurried off into the dark, taking the shortcuts and the side routes. Thirty minutes later, he was finally feeling a sense of the victory he felt entitled to in the first place.

This feeling was the consequence of more encounters with Barcelona fans on his way home. By the time he was home, he was feeling exhilarated again. With a thick stick he had picked up along the road, he had driven the point home to three male teenage fans he met along the road. They were wildly and loudly celebrating the victory of their club and had paid no attention to his menacing command that they stop their jubilant chatter. They thought he was hilarious.

He had swung the heavy stick wildly against them, crushing through flesh and bone and joint. His strength was inspired by his pain. His face was firm and solid as he dealt his fatal blows, blind to the cries and shrieks of his victims—the enemy.

He was a striker for the team. He was a striker for the Red.

He kept on striking until there was silence around him. Afterwards he had met another fan, a girl who had the audacity to wear a Barcelona jersey, strutting in her incongruous heels like the queen of the soccer field, as though—the pain had flared in his head.

He had ended her reign with a stone by the side of the path. The stone was heavy enough to do the job with a single blow. He threw it against her head like a football. She had crumpled to the ground, jersey and all. He had picked up the stone again and pounded her head continuously, until the once pretty face was a mess of bone, blood and hair.

But for now he felt good; it had been a fine conclusion to the evening after all. The battle on the pitch may have been lost, but the war was still on. He had offered his sacrifices to the devil lurking in his skull. He approached his house, and in the distance he heard the voice of his father loudly celebrating Barcelona's victory over his club.

His father's voice was drunk and boastful. "There is now a champion of Europe, friends. There is now a champion where formerly there were opponents. Drink and be merry, people, the Red Devils have been defeated!"

He walked faster, anxious not to meet his father this night. He would just slip in and sneak into his room. But in the front yard, there was his father, and other *ballist* friends, about thirteen of them.

They were celebrating the victory in grand style. Bottles of Star lager and Guinness stout were strewn on the table before them in varying stages of decline. The voices of the rowdy company kept on cheering his father's conceited speech. And as the cheering voices got louder, his headache returned.

He cursed.

But, finally, he knew what to do to stop the headache once and for all time.

The Red Devil had to be appeased.

He entered the main house unnoticed and, with a sense of wrongs about to be righted, he went into the kitchen, pulled out the utensil drawer in the cabinet, and grasped the pointed kitchen knife. The stainless steel edge gleamed in the fluorescent light as he brought the knife out of the cabinet. Then he went back outside towards the gathering where —.

Where the Red was being mocked by his father.

He grimaced as the headache pounded into his head with a vengeance.

This would be the biggest sacrifice of all.

A Nation Where Peace and Justice Reigns

(From *"The Anthem"*)

The Utopia that underlies this fantasy
Is that of a terrorist desiring amnesty.
It's possible, though. What hasn't been done?
But before that occurs, some things should be undone.
Peace is good for capitalist days,
When the stocks are high on the monitor's rays.
But ask the militant crouching by the swamp,
What is peaceful about living under a clamp?
If you want peace, then talk of due process,
And speaking of that, let's discuss justice.
Justice is the act of paying one's debt,
Giving each man his due and wealth.
Where is the justice in the Exclusive List?
When the central power holds all in its fist.
What do we say about the courts of law?
Truth still is: they're in the lion's paw.
'There ain't no justice there, it's back to the street;
Blow up a pipeline, beat a quick retreat.'

What is Peace? Let's enter the markets.
Not the exchange of equities in packets,
But the real one, home of sweat and sour smells.
The market woman with the *garri* she sells
Ask her for her version of Peace
Then go ahead, and ask about Justice.

She'll give you an account of her life;
First the budget balancing of the weary housewife,
Next, coping with children and the health issue.
Private clinics are not for her likes. Public? *Shoo!*
The same goes for getting education:
"They say that's how we'll build the nation.
I'm not educated, but my children will be,
That is all the wealth they'll get from me."
But where is the school she'll take them to?
The schools the Minister's children can never go?
The ones under the shed, the ones in the corner,
In houses forgotten by the town planner.
Is this Justice? She begs to disagree.
Oppression, certified with the highest degree.
"Here in the market, it's another matter.
You pay the local taxes; the chairman is getting fatter,
You also rent the shops from his younger sister.
Paul is robbing you, yet you still pay Peter!
And the market touts are just as bad."
She'll go on and on; this place is mad!

Here. We have another customer;
The ill-fated government worker
Who entered the civil service for lack of another.
What has he to say on our Justice matter?
Oh, he can't even answer, he's still under oath,
He's hurrying away, out of here fast.
Don't blame him much. You understand the fact:
Civil Service Rules, Official Secrets Act.

The ideals of nation building
(Once more to the wordy gilding)
Allow for lofty aims of peace and such,
But reality shows us this much:
Peace is just a fallacy by those at the top.
Justice—there's no such thing. Full stop.

THREE:
The Touts on the Bridge

"First they came for the Socialists, and I did not speak out—because I was not a Socialist. Then they came for the Trade Unionists, and I did not speak out—because I was not a Trade Unionist. Then they came for the Jews, and I did not speak out—because I was not a Jew. Then they came for me— and there was no one left to speak for me."

MARTIN NIEMOLLER

At a quarter past six, on a Saturday evening, Lawal locked the main entrance to the offices of Craig, Adele & Babatope (Estate Surveyors), on the fifth floor of the Churchill Towers on Marina Road in Lagos, and rode the lift down to the ground floor. Lawal noted that the regular front desk officers had since gone home. In their place, a tired-looking uniformed policeman sat at the reception desk and waved a half-hearted goodbye to him as Lawal exited the building. He walked round to the back of the building where his car sat forlornly in the middle of the parking lot.

He glanced upwards: only few businesses in the building were open this late on a Saturday. The few, lighted windows of the working offices stood out like the white squares of a crossword puzzle across the length of the 13 storeys. Having satisfied his idle curiosity, he turned his head and squinted into the evening sky, focusing on the silhouette of the Apongbon Link Bridge that stretched out against the evenly-lighted horizon. The cool orange sun was setting into the dusk. The cars on the bridge already had their rear-lights on, and the red pinpoints moving in a silent stream informed him that the Lagos Island traffic was just tolerable enough for him to join in and journey homewards to Surulere without much effort.

Lawal had spent most of the day cooped up in his cubicle, the solitary occupant of the entire floor, labouring over the technical points of a series of valuation reports. Weekend hours were a part of the sacrifices necessary to ensure his stable, middle class, income. But now that the day was darkening, he was in a hurry to get home.

He paused before his car dejectedly. He had bought the "second-hand" 1989 Opel Omega three years earlier and it had run its full course. In the last two weeks, it had been throwing a series of inexplicable tantrums, either stopping unexpectedly for no apparent reason, or failing to start at first try. He was worried about a sudden breakdown at this time of the day, on his way home. As he got into his car, he said a silent prayer before starting the engine. The car came to life and Lawal sighed unconsciously.

Three bridges linked the Lagos islands to the mainland. The Carter Bridge, constructed in 1901 was the oldest. It was first constructed by the colonialists for quick access from Ebute Metta to Lagos Island and later reconstructed by the military administration in the boom era of the '70s. The Third Mainland Bridge, the longest bridge in Africa, was an architectural marvel that spanned almost the entire length of the Lagos Lagoon: streaming traffic between the islands and the farthest points in the city. The Eko Bridge, the shortest of the three, was the direction in which Lawal was now headed.

Besides being worried about his car, Lawal was also nervous about the Eko Bridge's reputation. He had heard tales of the touts who lurked in the dark shadows of the bridge and pounced on helpless drivers, mercilessly dispossessing them of cash and property and—in some horrific instances—their lives. The touts' mode of operation, according to the gloomy stories, was to monitor the stranded car for a few minutes to be sure no immediate help was available. Once satisfied with the isolation of the victim, the touts would surround the car, and despite the presence of other cars whizzing past on the bridge, begin a regime of extortion on the hapless driver and passengers.

Lawal was not a valiant person by general standards. He had done his fair share of heroic actions, but "heroic" only by conceptual definition and not in physical terms. As a general rule, he avoided situations that could put him in physical danger, not out of timidity, but due to a highly refined instinct of self-preservation. He was the kind of person who would rather give in quietly to an assailant's demands than contest the impending deprivation of his property. It was the same approach to other forms of violent oppression: soldiers, policemen, and road touts. *It was better to bend over than to stand and fight.* For this reason, he was not eager to determine the veracity of the stories he had heard about the bridge. He only wanted to get home safe.

With serious doubts about his car's abilities, he manoeuvred the vehicle through the driveway and turned left into the one-way Marina Road. After driving a few meters he made a right turn as the road blended into the base of the Apongbon Link Bridge. The car seemed to hesitate at the climb, and the engine faltered slightly. Lawal shifted into second and then third gears, ramming his foot down into the accelerator while half-depressing the clutch in a bid to rev up the engine and boost the speed of the car. The tactic worked and the car picked up pace. He steadied the throb of the engine and then melted into the traffic on the left coming from Victoria Island. At the end of the bridge he went down the ramp into the valley of Apongbon Street.

As Lawal drove down the bridge, he entered his familiar state of *trafficophobia*—as he called it—the fear that strikes a commuting driver when he sees a long stretch of vehicles before him, stalled in traffic; and Lawal felt his bowels knot, as a shiver crawled up his spine.

Apongbon Street—a corrupted translation of *"the Scotsman with the Red Beard"*, so named in honour of William McCoskry, who had acted as Governor of the colony of Lagos in 1861—was a confused beehive of rowdy commercial and private vehicles, impatient commuters, shouting traders and hawkers, all scattered in a jumbled mass against the backdrop of the old buildings, tall and looming, covered in fading adverts of consumer products vying for visual attention as the day faded into night. The area had the usual assortment of unruly *danfo* buses with even more unruly conductors and touts obstructing traffic, creating a bottleneck that allowed only one vehicle to pass at a time. Lawal slowed down as he joined the stream of pressing cars inching through the valley.

The car shuddered as he shifted downwards and Lawal's confidence in the Omega's ability to push through the Apongbon traffic on first gear diminished significantly. Ahead in the distance, just a few metres away, was the wide and open stretch of the Eko Bridge, free of traffic and promising a fast getaway from the madness of the evening.

If only the car could make it through this damn traffic.

Night was falling fast over Lagos Island. The crowded mass of commuters waiting for buses at the valley of Apongbon Street were beginning to lose their distinct forms. Lawal pushed the car forward foot by foot, revving the engine at each pause in movement to prevent the car from stalling, even as he carefully weaved through the broken network of vehicles on the road. It was a delicate operation that required full concentration.

Several minutes later, the traffic was behind him. Relieved, though still anxious, he pushed down on the accelerator and the car surged towards the ascent of the Eko Bridge. But just as he was beginning to think his troubles were over, the car gave a sudden jerk, and a shiver of dread ran along Lawal's spine. Quickly, he switched gears and twitched his feet, maintaining pressure on both the accelerator and the clutch simultaneously, repeating the tactic he had used earlier at the rise of the Apongbon Link Bridge. His action did little to propel the car forward. The vehicle attempted a weak push, but the pressure required for it to climb the bridge was more than its engine could summon. Instead, it sputtered and rolled backwards to the bottom of the bridge before coming to a complete stop.

In the distance, the sun set beneath the horizon.

Lawal cursed. For a while, he sat in the car, desperately pressing down on the accelerator and turning the ignition repeatedly; trying to get it started again. Finally, he gave up. The car was dead.

Bastard!

Then quite suddenly, he remembered the infamous bridge touts and began to panic. His first thought was to roll up the windows of the vehicle and he did this hurriedly. His second thought was to hide his expensive smartphone that was lying atop the gearbox. He switched the phone off and flung it under his seat. Then it occurred to him that he would need to place a call to his mechanic. He hurriedly reached under his seat to recover the jettisoned device, but he discovered he could not retrieve it as easily as he had discarded it.

Damn! He must have thrown it too far.

The seat of the vehicle was low on the floor. He bent down and crouched, sweating, stretching his hands, blindly under his seat. The night was fast around him and the car was dark. Eventually, his hands found the phone and he clutched it in haste.

Then he heard a series of rapid knocks on the window of his car.

He looked up. His worst fears had materialised in the shape of two vaguely outlined figures standing on either side of the car. They kept on rapping on his windows, seemingly determined to speak to him.

Lawal's bowels roiled.

He dropped the phone again and raised his head from the base of the car, shakily summoning some false courage. He took his time adjusting into the driver's seat. Once settled, he rolled down the window on the driver's side, a tight expression on his face.

"Yes? What's the problem?"

"*Oga*, your car get problem? You need mechanic?" The man standing on the driver's side of the car was a short, squat fellow. Possibly in his early thirties, he was grinning cheerfully, displaying crooked teeth. Lawal thought the grin looked devious, the grin of a wolf circling its prey.

The other man came round to join his associate, he was taller and less facially expressive, but Lawal still deduced the impression of a mean character from the immobile visage. Both men were dressed in roughly similar clothes: faded, engine-oil stained shirts and dirty jean trousers, rolled to the ankles. They both stood over the window, their combined breath hard on Lawal's face.

"*Oga*, this place where you park no good at all," the first man continued. "Make we help you push your car go front small. If you stay here, these touts for bridge no go let you rest o."

Lawal looked at him incredulously. The man was suggesting that they were the good guys and the *real* touts were yet to come.

"So *wetin* you come want?" Lawal asked them.

"*Na* mechanic we be," the short man's grin was unrelenting. "We go help you fix am. *Na* only small money e go chop. *Na* injector dey worry am."

Lawal thought hard for a few seconds. From their clothes, the men *looked* like they dealt with vehicles habitually, maybe he was

lucky and they were genuine mechanics. It was no use being par-
anoid when he needed help. He opened the door and got out of
the car.

"*Oga, make we push this car comot for here o. By now, the touts for
don dey notice us. E better make we push am go on top bridge.*"

With that, the two men set out to work, pushing and steering the
car up towards the bridge. Lawal followed behind them, still hesitant
about the logic of pushing the car to the top of the bridge, away
from the seeming safety of the sprawling confusion in the Apongbon
valley. On the other hand, the men had a point, if the touts were to
spot him, they were likely to emerge from the night crowd gathered
in the valley; besides, every step forward took him closer home.

As soon as the men had pushed the car a fair distance from the
starting point, they stopped and waited for Lawal to join them. The
taller of the two sat on the boot of the car while the short man beck-
oned to Lawal, the grin still plastered on his face. Lawal thought him
too cheerful for the situation.

"*Oga,* how much you *wan'* pay us?" the short man asked.

Lawal had been expecting some demand for payment. There was
still no free lunch in Lagos, but he needed to know what services he
would be paying for.

"Which work exactly you *wan'* do for the car?"

The short man was eloquent as ever. Hurriedly, he described all
possible ailments that could be afflicting the vehicle and then several
more remedies. He was ready to go to town and get fuel, he said.
He was sure the fuel supply was being hampered in some way — or
maybe it was the battery. It was definitely not the injector, he revised
the earlier opinion, but it looked like the spark plugs would need
replacing. After a few minutes and a presentation befitting of an
experienced salesman, he demanded Ten Thousand Naira.

"What?" Lawal's hesitation was replaced by outrage.

"Do you think I carry around that kind of money?" Lawal had relapsed into proper English as he hurriedly responded to the men. "Ten Thousand is a lot of money to spend at short notice to fix a car! This is not money for house rent; it's just to restart a car. For God's sake, I'm just a typical worker; I rarely have up to Five Thousand Naira when I go around."

The tall man had not been smiling, but now he was definitely frowning. He got off the car and spoke for the first time, a low growl of a voice:

"So, you just *dey* waste our time since, *abi?*"

It's a simple question, not a threat. Lawal thought to himself, struggling to control a rising panic. *It's a simple question.*

Lawal spread his hands outwards, in a helpless gesture. The two men exchanged glances and he shivered slightly.

"How much *dey* your hand?" the short man asked. His grin was gone now.

The bridge seemed silent and indifferent despite the cars flashing past. No one seemed to take note of the incident occurring by the side of the road. Occasionally, a passenger in a vehicle would glance at them, seeing nothing; curious only in the same way that a baby is curious about a playful stranger. A mere instinctive reflex, ordinary and impersonal.

In the distance, far below the bridge, Lawal could see the city lights of the Lagos mainland dotted across the night.

"*Oga*, how much *dey* your hand?" the short man repeated. Lawal thought he heard a measure of menace in the voice.

"One Thousand Naira."

The short man considered this reply. "*Wey* your phone?"

"My phone? What for?"

"You fit call person *na*, call person make them bring money come. *Abi?*"

Suddenly, Lawal had a full comprehension. These men were irrational bastards and he had been attempting to deal with them on a rational level. There was no solution in that approach. They were here to extort from him and would do so at any cost. These were the touts on the bridge and he had finally met them. He wanted to laugh out. Now that he knew his opponents he felt peculiarly relieved.

The touts on the bridge.

"My phone is in my car. The phone battery is dead."

The grin came back again. "Ah, that's bad, *Oga*. Which phone *you dey use, na* Nokia?"

Trick question. Yes, you lose, No, you still lose.

"Yes."

"*Make we see am na*, we fit quickly go help you charge *am* under bridge."

Now Lawal was certain, he was the victim of a systematic robbery. *Well, no problem.* If they would take the phone and leave, he was fine with that. He moved towards the car and got inside. Feeling foolish about his earlier attempts to hide the phone he reached beneath his seat again to retrieve it.

Bastard car! He should be home now if not for this bastard car.

He found the phone and sat up.

A frown crawled up his face as he thought of his circumstances; a swell of anger at his own impotence was rising in him. For the first time for as long as he could remember, he was angry at the social and legal system that made him defenceless in the face of violence and yet encouraged the violence to be directed against him. But he was angrier at the vehicle. He hated the men outside his car, but he hated the car even more than anything else at that moment.

What more could he have done to keep the car in good shape? He had serviced it, cleaned it, done the bodywork and the bastard car still let him down at the worst possible moment.

Angrily, he turned the ignition again just to have a reason to hate the car more.

The car shuddered beneath him and the engine started.

The short man was the first to react to this unexpected turn. He dashed to Lawal's side; his face was an expression of surprise.

"Hey! *Oga*, the motor *don* start? Wait, you no go *fit comot* like that *o*."

Relief flooded through Lawal like tropical rain after a dry spell. He looked out at the short man who had once again leant against the car. The man's expression was forbidding. There was no grin.

"*Oga*, thank God say the car don start. *Oya settle us na*. Jus' bring the one thousand *wey dey* your hand, make we *dey* go."

The short man placed a hand on the steering wheel. His associate had also come forward and now stood silently before the car.

The anger that had been building up in Lawal burst out in force; directed now at the men who had interfered with his night.

"You're crazy." Lawal replied, "One Thousand Naira just because you pushed the car?" He then revved the accelerator as he shifted from neutral into first gear.

Seeing that Lawal was about to drive off, the short man swiftly grabbed hold of Lawal's left hand and then attempted to switch off the ignition. But his hold was not strong enough. Lawal twisted his arm out of the man's grip, shifted his gear to reverse and started to move out of the sidewalk and into the main road. His lights were still off and he had difficulty manoeuvring. Both men were chasing the car now, even as he reversed the vehicle furiously. The taller man was the more agile of the two, he got to Lawal's side quickly and, like his associate earlier did, he attempted to force Lawal's hand off the steering wheel.

I have had enough of this bullshit!

Lawal stopped reversing and changed to first gear. He moved the car forward a bit, the tall man still attempting to restrain him, then in a calculated move, Lawal veered the steering sharply while changing gears into a fast reverse. The motion caught the tall man by surprise. He was knocked off from the side of the car towards the road. He could not maintain his balance and he spiralled off, hitting the ground with a loud groan and a discernible thud. Lawal barely suppressed a smile as he thought of the man's fractured bones.

I will take control of what is mine.

Ahead, the short man stood still for a moment, as he watched his friend. Then his grin came back onto his face, and this time it was definitely malevolent. He trotted towards Lawal confidently. Lawal switched to first gear again, and began to drive towards the man dashing towards him. In a brief, fixed point in time and space, Lawal and the short man stared at each other from the distance between them, as though each man was daring the other to keep coming forward. Then Lawal pressed down on the accelerator, held a steady course, and ran straight into the short man.

I will not be intimidated.

The short man seemed poised to jump onto the hood of the car, and just at the moment of impact, he sprang. But he was not quick enough. The car got him in the knees and he fell back to the road. Lawal did not stop. He drove straight on, pushing the full weight of the vehicle over the now screaming man. The car juddered as all four wheels climbed over the inert body. Lawal savoured the crushing vibrations he felt beneath the car.

I will win.

From his rear-view mirror, Lawal could see the tall man attempting to get on his feet. Lawal reversed the vehicle, again climbing over the body of the short man, and rammed the back of the car into the tall man, gritting his teeth as he did so.

With the night covering his activity, he drove the car backwards and then forwards several times, climbing over the two bodies, consciously punishing the touts for all forms of aggression he had ever received from armed men and their masters. Every thud underneath the car was a song for justice in a bloody rhythmic dance of man and machine that continued for a while until, finally satisfied and purged of his anger, he returned to a gradual sanity.

Finally, Lawal drove on and the vehicle blended into the night like a black box, slowly picking up pace until it was moving just as fast as the other cars on the bridge. Lawal focused on the road before him, he deliberately ignored his rear-view mirror, which still reflected the receding image of two inert bodies on the bridge.

The City At Night

The moon doesn't shine on this city.
The sky is a darkened glass
Sheeted over overreaching spires.
We stretch out our eyes—rooftops everywhere.
The neon lights are a pale copy
Of nature's sweeping lucent.

But you and I can steal a retreat,
Row across the lagoon beneath the dark expanse.
And hopefully, far away from the gloomy high-rise,
We'll catch a glimpse of the sweet full moon.

FOUR:
There is More Than Meets the Eye

Now the day is over,
Night is drawing nigh,
Shadows of the evening
Steal across the sky.

CHRISTIAN HYMN

There is a long stretch of asphalt between the Yaba and Oyingbo markets in central Lagos. Known by the flattering designation "Murtala Mohammed Way", it has been around for as long as Lagos itself has existed. Although it was little more than a bush path for traders in the late colonial period, it had matured into an important highway, linking a focal area of the mainland to the islands beyond. The road also saw some good times in the 1980s; it had endured the crisis-ridden wear and tear of the 1990s and had now been resuscitated to a more dignified form at the turn of the millennium.

Every day, the road delivers a one-way stream of traffic from Yaba to Oyingbo in a continuous torrent of commercial and private vehicles. *Danfo* buses swerve in impatiently at its intermittent bus stops, with their irascible conductors half hanging out of the doors, waving passengers in and shouting the names of bus stops upfront: *Alagomeji! Adekunle! Office!* while the private cars dash onwards to Oyingbo and the Carter Bridge further ahead.

On the right side of the road, when facing towards Oyingbo, the compound of the Railway Corporation borders the road with a stretch of ancient walls. On the left side of the road are the spaced entrances into the colonial layout of old Yaba and Ebute Metta East—a crisscross pattern of streets whose activities are hidden from the road. The entrances to the streets are flanked by the walls of private compounds, the occasional petrol filling station and carwash, a couple of churches and some other nondescript buildings. Because it stretches between two major markets, there is usually little commercial activity along the road—apart from a few roadside traders. A person walking the length of the road would have little company.

When the sun begins to set, the homeward traffic gathers on the road in tight embrace for an hour or two, as vehicles struggle to exit Oyingbo Market to either turn around and loop back towards the mainland or proceed towards the islands. Once the traffic deadlock loosens, the night settles in and the road goes to sleep.

In the dark, there is more than meets the eye and the road takes on a different mien. The Railway Corporation walls loom forbiddingly like a primeval barricade, casting dark shadows on the sidewalks, and hiding even more shades along its edges. Human movement thins to nothingness and the walk for any night crawler unlucky enough to have missed the last of the *danfo* buses from Yaba is even lonelier. The slumber of the road is disturbed only by the sporadic passage of the occasional car and the silent cries of sacrificial victims. Only the very brave walk the length of the road without a shiver.

On one of such nights, when the evening lay still and the shadows of the Railway Compound hung over the road, Michael, a young man in his mid-thirties, walked along the road as he began his homeward journey towards Oyingbo. A clothes trader at the Yaba market, Michael ordinarily took the last bus to get home. However, in the last couple of weeks, he had developed the habit of making the long trek instead. The walk gave him time and a quiet atmosphere to sort out his thoughts. He was not a happy man.

His wife of six years was dying in the village, and time was running out on the option left to save her life—the one that he had to think about. His two sons were living away from him, as he could not look after them by himself. Although he had been agonising over his wife's health in the past six months, only in the last few days had a way to save her really begun to crystallise in his thoughts.

The road was long and empty except for Michael and a young woman who was walking ahead of him. She walked rapidly, her gown brushing against her heels routinely as she treaded against the night breeze. This was the fourth night they were sharing the road alone. Their travel had become patterned; she would catch up with him just after the Yaba market, and then walk on ahead of him into the distance. He had seen her a few times in the market. She sold food—late-night meals—to the tired bus drivers and the traders who shut down the night market. Initially, she was no more than a welcome distraction from the thoughts that plagued him, but now she had become a familiar landmark, as natural to his trek as the occasional vehicles that lit up the road at intervals. He had become conversant with the rhythm of her movement; her lithe steps stressed the gentle curvature of her posterior. She was small in frame, but a fast walker. A spark of life in the dead of the night. Michael had never caught up with her before—not that he had ever wanted to. He marvelled at her confidence in the gloom, the self-assuredness of her movements, seemingly certain that the stretch of road, dark and lonely as it was, posed no threat to her.

Michael himself was not a brave man. His first effort at walking the road after dark had been a stern test of his self-control, for at every startling noise, he had almost broken into a run. He had journeyed cautiously, looking around him for signs of unusual activity, and constantly looking back to be sure he was not being followed. There was no safe road at night. It was not just thieves and robbers he was worried about, but also bloodsuckers—ghouls inspired by urban legends—and kidnappers. Michael was extremely credulous, and he believed in a world that posed a thousand dangers to the unwary. Not long ago, a deranged football fan in this area had run amok in the night, killing people at random after a match. It was on nights like this that the men of the dark plied their dreadful trade and Michael was unwilling to be a buyer.

After his first night on the route, he had become a little less apprehensive about the dangers of the darkness, but he still kept a wary eye open. Even now, as he hurried on behind the girl in the flowing gown, he walked with his mind alert to the environment; his left hand tightly clutching at the strap of his bag, his body moving sharply in a constant effort to prevent his senses from becoming too relaxed even as he waded through his thoughts. He walked on behind the girl, her dark outline a consoling presence in the middle of the night.

His wife had been diagnosed with cancer six months ago and now she lay dying in her father's house. "Cancer" was what the Lagos doctors called it, but the village native medicine man had spat the word out in disgust. *Cancer? What cancer? This is the handiwork of your enemies. They are jealous of your success. You will need to be vigilant and strong if she is to survive this.*

It had been a long road to the village medicine man's hut; if the, surprisingly, very modern bungalow could be called a hut. Despite their Pentecostal brand of Christianity, Michael and his family had had no problems consulting the traditional healer. Besides, his pastor's advice had been along similar, if parallel, lines: *She can be cured, but only by fasting and prayer.* The fasting had been easy but the prayer was useless, and eventually, the government hospital discharged his wife and recommended private care for her. Private care was expensive, and Michael, though he had a profitable business with two employees, was not wealthy. After the money spent on expensive drugs had failed to produce any significant improvement, his wife's family had come for her and taken her back to the village. Their two children had gone to stay with his sister while Michael shuttled between the village and Lagos, desperately seeking an elusive cure while also trying to earn the money to pay for it.

He had finally turned to the idea of consulting a native doctor; on several nights, he had sat beside his wife's bed, urging her to drink from repellent concoctions made from herbs and other nondescript ingredients. He would have gladly swallowed these himself if it would have eased her pain. But still, there had been no signs of improvement in his wife's health and Michael had begun to give in to the despair of watching her die until his father had called him aside three weeks earlier. And, during what he called a "man-to-man" talk, he had advised Michael on the way forward.

☙❧

Now as he began the last leg of his trek, Michael considered his father's advice and his heartbeat quickened along with his pace.

The gods will accept a life for a life.

It was a paradigm which he understood and which he had never questioned. His wife could have her life but only in exchange for another.

In this life, there is more than meets the eye.

His father had refused to say more, but had handed him over to the medicine man—who had carefully outlined the items needed and what Michael was required to do.

He had agonised over the decision he needed to make in search of a justifiable rationale and the frustration had driven him almost to a state of mental paralysis. *How does a man reconcile a contradictory proposition? How does a man maintain a principle and still avoid the consequences of its implementation?* The nightly walks from Yaba to Oyingbo had been a search for sanity. But now, as a desperate requirement, the decision had come to him, along with an opportunity for its execution. He was ready to lose his soul. He was prepared to push his own limits, as long as his wife would be saved.

In the far distance, the pinpoints of the Oyingbo Market lights were beginning to show, but around him on Murtala Mohammed Way, the night lay dark and quiet. This was the kind of night when kidnappers and bloodsuckers lurked in the shadows and innocent blood became the feast of the nocturnal, Michael thought, as he began to feel a tightening in his stomach.

Again, he looked ahead at the young woman and wondered where she got the courage to walk the length of the road. It was almost suicidal, the way she walked the night. It was as if she was daring danger, urging it to ensnare her. This perception of her vulnerability was heightened by her fragile frame; she did not appear capable of defending herself in a physical conflict. Michael wondered if she had parents or a husband who let her stay out so late, or if she was an independent girl, living alone. He frowned at this thought; he didn't like women who lived alone.

Before him, the girl increased her pace—as though aware of his thoughts, and the distance between the two walkers increased. Michael took even longer steps, intent on catching up with her.

As soon as he was almost behind her, Michael slowed down so as not to alarm the girl. He walked on gently behind her for a few seconds, observing the outline of her back while he withdrew the object in his bag. If she sensed the proximity of her night companion, she did not show it. She walked on purposefully, eager to complete her night's journey. Michael considered her briefly before he acted.

In a swift, rehearsed motion, he swung the machete that he had withdrawn from his bag upwards and slashed at the girl's neck from behind. Time stood still for him as her torso wavered slightly before falling to the ground. Her decapitated head bounced off her shoulders and rolled off the sidewalk, stopping just at it got onto the road, a trail of blood tracing out its path. Michael crouched to retrieve it. He quickly deposited it into his bag, almost shamefully, without looking at it, and then he hurried off into the night.

☙❧

There is a long stretch of asphalt between the Yaba and Oyingbo markets in central Lagos and in the dark, there is more than meets the eye and the road takes on a menacing mien. The walls along the road loom forbiddingly like a primeval barricade, casting dark shadows on the sidewalks, and hiding even more shades along its edges. Human movement thins to nothingness and the walk for any night crawler unlucky enough to have missed the last of the buses is even lonelier. The slumber of the road is disturbed only by the sporadic passage of the occasional car and the silent cries of sacrificial victims. Only the very brave walk the length of the road without a shiver.

The Hyperlinks You Gave Me Went For A Swim

Yesterday,
Silky bands of ideas and knowledge
Encircled us in close commune
All that you said was
True.

Today,
Flying a bike alone on the Eko Bridge
I looked to the Lagoon
And it was—
Blue.

FIVE:
The Bombing of the Third Mainland Bridge

God's blessing on the architects who build
The bridges o'er swift rivers and abysses
Before impassable to human feet.

HENRY WADSWORTH LONGFELLOW, THE COVERED BRIDGE AT LUCERNE

*"All praise and thanks is for to God, Creator,
Owner, Sustainer of the Worlds. The Entirely
Merciful, The Especially Merciful."*

THE QURAN

Repair Work Begins on Third Mainland Bridge

R epair work has commenced on the Third Mainland Bridge today. The Third Mainland Bridge, which was completed in 1990, is the longest and most important of the three bridges linking the Lagos Mainland to the Lagos islands. According to the supervisor in charge of the project, Engineer Rilwan Akindele, the repairs are long overdue and are being conducted for public safety. Speaking with our correspondent, yesterday, Engineer Akindele stated that although the decision to commence work on the bridge by the Federal Government was a sudden one, it was not unexpected. Diversion of traffic on the bridge has since commenced...

Body Count Rises to 120 As Boko Haram Strikes In Jos

Terrorist group, Boko Haram, yesterday claimed responsibility for the recent attack in Jos that left over 100 people dead and an unspecified number injured. The group has been responsible for a series of deadly attacks in the north, through bombs and random shootings. The Presidency has set up a committee to tackle the issue of security and unrest in the north of the country, the Boko Haram main area of operations...

(Excerpts from the Guardian Newspaper, July 9.)

Email from Rilwan Akindele to Shellong Kut. (Courtesy of Mr. Kut.)

From: rilwan.akindele@yahoo.co.uk
To: Skut@gmail.com
Date: July 9
Subject: Re: Hello

Oga Shellong,

My apologies for not seeing you before I left Abuja. I wanted to express my concern over the safety of your family in Jos personally. Unfortunately, the instruction to travel to Lagos came suddenly and I could not reach you on phone. I have been given the task of supervising the repair work on the Third Mainland Bridge in Lagos. You will recall that I spoke about this possibility the last time we saw. I'm so glad to be able to visit the bridge again. My wife is thoroughly miffed, but I know she is proud—like women usually are.

Speaking of the bridge, I stood on it today, my eyes sweeping across the horizon of the lagoon, and the only thought I had was that God must be proud of us humans for creating such magnificent works—for it is in the act of creation that we emulate God the most. Animals can destroy at will, but only humans can create purposefully and beyond instinct. Don't let me digress. I hope your family is safe. I will attempt to call you as soon as I can free myself from the several meetings I am currently involved in. My regards to Madam.

Rilwan.

⚓

Encrypted email message retrieved from the Inbox of faroukv@arrh.net. (Courtesy of the Nigeria State Security Service.)

From: shehuv@arrh.net
To: faroukv@arrh.net
Date: July 9
Subject: Preparations

Farouk, my brother,

The mercies of Almighty Allah, Lord of Worlds, be upon you. I have sent our brother, Saheed, to join you in Lagos, as I am unable to come myself. There is much work to be done here, but I will receive your reports myself. The Council has met and decided. It is time to strike the fat belly of Lagos as we take the Jihad to the south—the hypocritical self-seeking ones among us who caused confusion in our midst to safeguard their businesses in the city have been purged. You may know of some of these traitors: Imam Wahab, Seidou the

Blacksmith, and Rahman. They were blindfolded and beheaded before the brethren at the commandment of Our Great Leader.

Proceed as planned. The target remains the Third Mainland Bridge. Remember, the charges should be lined from one end of the bridge to another. Install them at night, and check them by day. The bridge must fall. We will send more brothers to Lagos to help you as soon as their camouflage training is complete.

Our brothers in the Ministry of Works have initiated the repair works that will give us cover to set up the charges. Saheed has been provided with the technical details of the bridge to help your work and the cash for necessary purchases. Communicate by phone only if you must. Avoid detection. May Almighty Allah and Our Great Leader be with you.

Your brother, Shehu.

Excerpt from Engineer Akindele's logbook of November 14. (Courtesy of Mrs. Akindele.)

General Report: Final check on the Adekunle end of 3MB today. Tests show that the vibrations have been fully resolved. [**Redacted Text**] Repair work should be concluded by the weekend. Quality Control Supervisor is prepared to sign off the papers. [**Redacted Text**] Meeting with EPA official postponed till November 16.

Memo: Saw the strange looking man on the main axis of the bridge this evening. I am uncomfortable with his presence on the bridge during a repair period. He is definitely not one of the workers. Again, he ran away as soon as I called out to him. If I come across him again, I will have to confront him.

Encrypted email message retrieved from *Sent Items* of
faroukv@arrh.net. *(Courtesy of the Nigeria State Security Service.)*

From: faroukv@arrh.net
To: shehuv@arrh.net
Date: November 16
Subject: Re: Preparations

My brother, the blessings of Almighty Allah and Our Great Leader be upon you. Our brothers have laid the charges and the work is complete. We await the command of Our Great Leader and the Council. I am honoured to have been given the task of bringing down this infidel structure. As planned, I will standby in a canoe beneath the bridge, around the middle of the stretch. I humbly suggest nightfall, to reduce the possibility of any rescue effort. By the time we are done, I promise you, not a single stone of that bridge will be left standing. As you may have seen in the news, I have had to inflict justice on the supervising engineer. He stumbled on me as I was examining the charges and he tried to tackle me. I must confess I took delight in telling him how his bridge would be destroyed before throttling him and throwing him into the water. So he is dead now and can be no trouble to our work.

Supervising Engineer Found Dead in Lagos Lagoon

The body of Engineer Rilwan Akindele was fished out yesterday from the Lagos Lagoon. Police sources confirmed that he died after falling off the Third Mainland Bridge. The coroner ruled the death as an accident. Until his death, Engineer Akindele was the supervisor of the on-going repair works on the Third Mainland Bridge. The repairs had commenced in July this year and the work is expected to be completed by the end of this month. He is survived by a wife and four children. Friends of the late engineer who spoke to Punch *described him as a fearless man who had been known to risk his life on several occasions to help other people. The Federal Government has expressed regrets over the loss and has promised to compensate the family of the deceased.*

(*Excerpt from* Punch Newspaper, *November 16.*)

Third Mainland Bridge Closed Again as Anti-Bomb Unit Sweeps Over

In a surprising development, the Inspector General of Police has ordered the immediate closure of the Third Mainland Bridge. Although official reasons have not been given for the closure, bomb disposal units were yesterday seen on the bridge. Confirming the suspicion of explosives being planted on the bridge, police sources say they were alerted to the possibility of a planned terrorist attack on the bridge after a detonator was recovered from the body of a suspected terrorist, identified as Farouk Wahab. The corpse surfaced on the lagoon on the morning of November 18. According to our sources, the police units have already disarmed several bombs. There was no clear indication of how the said terrorist drowned in the lagoon, but sources say his boat capsized. We were also reliably informed that the raid conducted two days ago on a suspected *Boko Haram* hide-out discovered in Akoka, Yaba, was made possible through the house address on a business identity card found on the corpse. The police raid led to the killing of six members of the terrorist group and the arrest of about 20 others.

Repair work on the Third Mainland Bridge was scheduled for completion this month. The bridge had been partially closed since July.

In an unrelated incident, the body of the supervisor previously in charge of the repairs on the bridge, Engineer Akindele, who died last week, was again recovered from the Lagos Lagoon two days ago. The mortuary where the corpse had previously been deposited had earlier reported that the body was missing. The deceased's family released a statement yesterday to the effect that they found this "prank by unknown persons" to be "distasteful and distressing". In the words of the deceased's brother, Yusuf Akindele, who spoke to our reporters, *"Why would anyone steal a dead body and throw it in the lagoon?"*

(Excerpt from the front page of Guardian Newspaper, *November 22.)*

Excerpt from the transcript of an interview with Nicholas Ogba on Channels Television. Recorded November 26. (Courtesy of Channels Television.)

Interviewer: Thank you very much for joining us on the show today, Nicholas. You recently posted a strange incident on your blog that has been generating a lot of buzz on the internet. For the benefit of our audience, can you tell us what happened on the night of the incident you reported?

Nicholas: Well, it was, *erm*, like you said, all kinds of strange. But, I have two or three people who can bear witness to this. It happened on Saturday night, around 8p.m., on the 17th. I can't forget the date. Myself and the boys, four of us, were all, like, you know, chilling by the lagoon front, at Unilag, just shooting breeze and talking stuff. We'd had, like, enough drinks, so everything was kind of, like, fuzzy. But anyway, we were all chilling and hanging out under the almond trees and savouring the lagoon view. You know, everything looks like poetry when you've had a few drinks. We'd been there for almost an hour when suddenly, a man rushed into our midst from nowhere shouting that he needed a canoe to take him under the bridge. He looked rough and haggard, like someone who had just escaped from prison. The boys teased him, but there was something about him that struck me as wildly serious. So I told him he could get a boatman downstream and I offered to search for one with him. So, we walked down along the lagoon for a while and we found a boatman willing to row him across. Then he asked me if I would come along with him on the ride and I said yes.

Interviewer: Why did you agree to this?

Nicholas: I don't know. I honestly don't know. Maybe it was the booze, or maybe it was the urgency of it all. But we got into the canoe and we started to row across. It was cold and the lagoon seemed to whisper dreadful things. But the man seemed unfazed; he only kept scanning around the water while urging the boatman to paddle faster towards the bridge. Then suddenly, he pointed out another canoe in the distance and told the boatman to head in that direction. I looked towards the distance and saw that there was a man sitting in the other canoe, looking up at the bridge as if monitoring traffic. Then our man tells the boatman to quietly take us close enough to the other boat so he can get in while we row away as fast as possible. The boatman does this and as soon as we are close, the man springs from the boat, nearly capsizing us, and jumps into the other boat. As our boatman starts to row away fast, I look behind and see the two men struggling until their boat fades off in the night.

Interviewer: Did you find out the identity of this stranger?

Nicholas: I did not know him then, but when I saw his picture on the Internet the next day, I recognised him instantly. It was one of those sensational stories on these gossip blogs. The story was about a celebrity corpse that had gone missing from a mortuary. I am not superstitious. I swear it. But the man who had accosted us that night and who fought the other man in the canoe was the engineer! The man who was said to have drowned in the lagoon days earlier!

Abiola Talks to God

I know you say I've done my part
But all I stood for rots in the past.
New names, great unknowns
Now feed of my buried bones.
Yes, they name me a few streets,
Schools, stadiums — tawdry treats.
Yes, maybe I get a profound date
In the calendar for history to relate
The tales of the struggle I went through.
Tell me, what I should construe
From the way things are today?
My bones lie where they lay
But my spirit fleets in dismay.
This is not the way I thought it would be,
This is not the future I cried to see.
These are not the people I died to give
My hopes. These are those who live
Off my sweat. How do you forgive?

SIX:
The Injustice of It All

"Those who can make you believe absurdities,
can make you commit atrocities."

VOLTAIRE

The nuances of the private and professional life of Dr. Tunde Olaoye were not an issue for me until the day I was walking down the corridors of the faculty of Social Science, my fingers and attention on my phone's keypad, and I bumped into the head of the Sociology department, Professor Helen Bankole.

"Sorry ma!" I exclaimed, with the right amount of culturally required contrition.

As usual, I had been typing on my mobile phone, discussing upcoming wedding parties, clothes, and other subject matters appropriate for a couple of twenty-two year old girls with my close friend, Simbo—a science student. I pocketed the phone hurriedly and smiled sheepishly at the older woman.

Professor Bankole accepted my apology in her usual gracious manner and proceeded on her course. A few steps later though, I heard her call my name.

"Lynda, wait a minute."

I turned back to face her, wondering what had crossed her mind. I wondered what sort of assignment she had for me. As the assistant class representative of the third year students, I was always getting tasks from lecturers, most of who considered student officials to be their personal slaves. However, Professor Bankole was a decent sort, and she only gave me serious stuff to handle. So I waited patiently while the professor considered her words.

"Are you aware of a certain rumour involving a senior staff of the department?" Professor Bankole asked in her firm and steady manner.

"No, ma. I'm not sure I know of any such rumour." It was an unusual question and I had no idea what she was hinting at.

The Professor cocked her head and stared at me sceptically before continuing.

"The rumour concerning Dr. Olaoye."

"Definitely not, ma." I protested my ignorance more firmly.

"Don't give me that innocent look, Lynda. I know you too well," the professor snapped. "I have strong reasons to believe that the messy situation originated from your class. I want you to get to the bottom of the story and find out the people who initiated the rumour. Ours is a responsible department. We are not running a breeding ground for character assassins and backstabbers. The Dean is anxious to resolve this issue and I want you to give me an oral report by the end of the week. Now, get going."

With that dismissal, the Velvet and Iron Lady of the department went her way, leaving me more than a little confused.

Dr. Olaoye taught Social Psychology to the third year class. He was a short, quick-tempered man who believed that there was no person capable of teaching his course more effectively than himself, and that only a few students had the natural ability to pass it. As he liked to point out in class, only a genius could get an A in his course, and he didn't believe there was more than one genius in any given environment—otherwise it defeated the definition of the word.

I had my first contact with him when, at the beginning of the second semester, I had stormed into his office to complain about my result in his course. I had been given an *E*, a grade that, despite my carefree approach to academics, I had never scored in any course until then.

On that day, as soon as I entered his office, he had given me a good going-over, pointedly inspecting me from head to toe, and then nodded with a smile.

I didn't go to his office to flaunt my physical virtues, but I admit that I thought myself quite striking that day. Of course, there were whispers that the man was an avid connoisseur of the fair sex, and I had decided to use that information to fair advantage. So I stood akimbo in front of his desk and furiously complained at the injustice of it all.

"Sir, it is not possible for me to fail your course. All my other results are *As* and *Bs*. Can you please take a look at my script again, sir? I'm really sure of this."

He leaned back on his chair and laughed out.

"What's your name, young woman?"

"Lynda Okorie."

"Take a seat, Lynda. Don't stand over me."

I was surprised at his response. I had expected, and prepared myself for a fight. But with his amiable attitude, I had taken a seat in front of his desk and affected a frown instead.

"So, Lynda, why do you think you cannot fail my course?"

"Because I'm not a dull student, sir. I do very well generally. An E is way below me."

"Of course, you are not a dull student. Nobody is." He laughed again.

I didn't think the remark was funny. Instead, I had brought out my historical statements of results from my handbag and showed them to him. He had scrutinised the papers, all the while smiling and nodding his head.

"Okay, I admit that you seem to be a good student, Lynda. I will give your script another look. However, don't expect a better result. I rarely make mistakes with my marking. Besides, don't let one result give you much worry. You can prove me wrong next semester. Right?"

His attitude had subdued my anger, and even though he did not remedy my result, I had developed an easy lecturer-student relationship with him afterwards. I had come to discover that the "*King of Soc-Psych*" was, outside the classroom, quite different from the smouldering façade that he portrayed during his lectures. I often called in at his office to have a chat with him on diverse issues—from a physical headache to profound talks on the state of the nation.

Unlike other lecturers who had acquired reputations for sexually harassing their female students, Dr. Olaoye never harassed anyone, at least none that I know of. After all, he never made a pass at me—except on one occasion, but I'll get to that later—and he never deliberately failed anybody. As a general rule, he failed *everybody*. He was reputed, however, to have a soft spot for the ladies and his favourites were usually assured good enough grades in the courses he taught.

Although it was also whispered in the dark corners of the faculty that his favour could be bought by an amorous night in his company or a wad of naira notes, I never attempted to remedy my first semester result with that currency, and neither was I bothered by the rumours of his dalliances with some of the female students. When it came to handling the male of the species, my motto has always been "live and let live" in deference to the generally acknowledged axiom that men would be men.

So when the HOD gave me her queer mandate, I was more perplexed than surprised. A few days earlier, I had been with Dr. Olaoye in his office and we had chatted amiably. He was his usual half-serious, half-mocking self and when I had asked how he was, he had replied in true fashion: "By turns well-behaved, mischievous, excited, randy, inspired, tired and depressed, but otherwise, generally fine."

I walked up the five floors of the faculty building to the staff offices, the effort of the exercise eased by the concentration of my thoughts. The background buzz of chattering students had diminished as I climbed higher and became conscious that I was close to my destination. I walked to Dr. Olaoye's door, and I did as the notice on the door instructed: KNOCK ONCE AND ENTER.

He was seated at his desk, his back hunched as he scrutinised some examination scripts he had been grading. Second semester exams were still in progress and most lecturers didn't start marking their scripts until after the exams. By university custom, this period was when lecturers fled the academic confines of the campus and attended to other pursuits. I waited quietly, leaning against the door, until Dr. Olaoye looked up.

"Yes, what can I do for you, Lynda?" He asked brusquely. His face was frozen in rigid disapproval like an ascetic who had found himself in a brothel.

This was not his usual form of greeting. In the past, I would have been entitled to a jovial variation of the phrase "Lynda girl, how far?"

"Nothing in particular," I muttered.

He gave me an exasperated look, as if trying to understand why his time was being wasted for no apparent reason.

"Well, in that case you may leave my office, please."

Well, well, I thought as I closed the door of his office behind me, *that was it.* No explanations, no assurances of future welcome; talk of getting the cold shoulder—I had been properly served. Suddenly, I felt humiliated. When a lecturer with whom you're friends tells you to *get out* of his office, it's a demotion you just don't shrug away. Whatever had gotten to the man, it had hit him quite badly, and since I had now been personally affected, I had to get to the root of the problem. Carrying out the HOD's instructions was not just for her satisfaction alone; it was for my bruised ego as well.

By the time I got out of the faculty building, I was feeling better. Having made a decision, I could focus on an action plan. A brisk walk took me to my hostel within ten minutes. It was six in the evening and there was time for me to fish for a little gossip before setting out again to study in the lecture rooms.

Once in my room, I grabbed a quick meal, and having satisfied the day's gastronomic needs, I went for a shower and then slipped into more comfortable clothes before going in search of any of my female classmates who might be around in the hostel. Girls do not lounge in their rooms in the evenings, not when there were men and boys to give them a good time. I hoped I would run into someone who was social enough to be informed of the latest campus gossip, but not popular enough to have a date for the evening. I met with success in the first room I called on.

Her name was Tola and given half the chance, she was quick to regale a listener with indiscreet stories of her working class boyfriend as well as other girls' lovers. She was a handy source of inside information on almost everything and anybody worth discussing. On a normal day, I steered clear of her company, but this wasn't a normal day.

"So, Tola," I began brightly, "What's been happening in the department that I've been missing? I've been hearing stuff about Dr. Olaoye. Tell me, are they true?" Of course I had absolutely no idea about anything, but while it was not a virtue to be regarded and avoided as a *busybody*; it was also not complimentary to be considered an ignoramus, especially by campus inferiors, like Tola.

Cheerfully ignorant of my private thoughts about her, Tola was only too eager to enlighten me on the lecturer's saga, although not in as straightforward a fashion as I would have scripted it. She was constantly running off tangent, asking irrelevant questions and providing me with unsolicited information on unrelated events and occasionally going off track for several minutes before I prompted her back to my area of interest.

Sans interpolations, the story I got from Tola was this: It seems that four days earlier, Dr. Olaoye had been in his office playing amorous host to a final year female student who visited him ostensibly to discuss her results. The chat had led to more serious negotiations between lecturer and student and soon they were engaged in passionate acts, traditionally and wisely confined to the bedroom. The wisdom behind the use of a bedroom was soon realised by the two contractors, for at an intense moment, the Dean of the Faculty had walked right in.

Now the Dean was one of those people who preached against vice in everyone but indulged in it themselves, he was generally considered a loud-mouthed hypocrite and it did not help that he always began his classes by quoting from the bible. His favourite mantra was that a lot of the problems attempted to be solved by the social sciences had been answered by the bible, and brandishing a small pocket-sized copy, he would point to it as the book made for everyone. He had often professed a desire for morning assemblies in the faculty, as was done in secondary schools, so that the students could say prayers and sing hymns before the day's work began. But even dogs can be spiritually inclined; and he was treated as a joker by everyone, but feared nonetheless. It was an unlucky person who fell afoul of his rules. He would dispense cruel justice with the expression of a man who has no choice in the matter. He disapproved of most of the lecturers, but truly and thoroughly disliked Dr. Olaoye.

Consequently, the Dean considered walking into Dr. Olaoye *in flagrante delicto,* a heaven sent opportunity to pronounce a long awaited judgment on the lecturer. On the Dean's instigation, Dr. Olaoye was scheduled to appear before the University Senate's Disciplinary Committee for a decision on the matter.

That, in brief, was the story Tola told me, and the one that had been circulating in the faculty.

Tola also told me, with hesitant laughter, that, well, no one had *actually* seen anything official to that effect nor had the facts been confirmed by the faculty authorities, but the story was making the rounds, and *anyway*, there's no smoke without fire, and the student body was not exactly depressed by the downfall of the King of Soc-Psych.

I was worried by the tale Tola told me. It had the ring of a cock-and-bull story; Dr. Olaoye was too smart to *get down* with a student in his office without locking his door—unless, maybe, he had become careless.

Also, the day of the alleged intrusion by the Dean was also the day of the incident I spoke of earlier—the first and only time Dr. Olaoye made a pass at me. On that day, I had been in the office with him sometime in the afternoon, seated at his desk listening to him give me a lesson in general politics. He was standing above me pontificating, when suddenly, he flicked off some speck from my cheeks and followed this up with a half-hearted attempt to kiss me on the lips.

Strangely, I had felt flattered, but I had pushed him away firmly. He had laughed heartily and asked me in his lecturer tone if he couldn't be allowed to give his "niece" a peck.

"In public, maybe, not in private, sir." I had replied, also laughing; and the episode was closed.

Now, having heard Tola's tale, I wondered how to get to the origin of this new story. Clearly, it was not factual; otherwise the HOD would not have sent me scouting around. I needed to get the girl alleged to have been with the lecturer.

"Do you know the girl involved?" I asked Tola.

"I don't know her personally, but I have seen her around in the faculty. In fact, Goke pointed her out to me today. Anyway, did you hear of the girl that committed suicide in the Lagoon—?"

I waved her off before she launched into more gossip and went in search of Goke, one of the class jesters. His antics varied from mimicking lecturers to playing practical jokes on other classmates. I pinned him down in front of his hostel and got to speak with him. I was quite certain he originated the story, but he swore gravely that he knew nothing of its origins, but that he considered it gospel truth.

"But the HOD wants me to fish out the source," I told him, "Why would she send me on a wild-goose chase?"

"Sweetheart," he shook his head in mock sympathy, "You're just a tool for the faculty's cover-up of the event. You have to wake up, baby. Don't be fooled by the Machine!"

I ignored his mockery and concentrated on my objective. "So, Tola says you know the girl. Who is she?"

"Well, I'm not sure if the girl I pointed out to Tola is the girl, *sha*. *Actually*, it was Yemi 'Yellow' who suggested that she was the one. But based on certain assumptions which I will not trouble you with, I believe that she *could* be the one."

I rolled my eyes at him and went in search of Yemi "Yellow".

Yemi "Yellow", another of the class clowns, was no more helpful than Goke was, and I spent the rest of the week going from "someone" to "someone" while carefully avoiding Dr. Olaoye's path. Those I talked to confirmed the story but really could not remember how or where they had first heard it. I understood the machinery of school gossip well enough; it wasn't so much a case of suspects withholding information as it was of looking for one person in a crowded market — the information was there, but the bustle and jostle of campus life made it difficult to reach. Unfortunately, students had already started moving out of the hostels for the sessional holidays and my sources for further information had begun to reduce.

So by the end of the week, I was forced to give up my fruitless investigation and go to the HOD's office to report myself. She was squinting into her computer's screen and barely looked up at me as I explained my failure.

When I was done talking, she looked up.

"The Dr. Olaoye matter? Oh, don't bother about that anymore," she said. She paused for a while, as though considering what to tell me. "I should have told you this earlier; Dr. Olaoye has resigned from the faculty staff. He has taken a job in a private university outside the state. Apparently, his wife—a nasty woman from what I hear—got wind of the rumour and left him, taking their two children with her."

The Velvet and Iron Lady looked tired. "Poor man, I guess he had it coming," and then she dismissed me.

Later on, after my conversation with the HOD, I called the president of the department's student body in a bid to make sense of the news the HOD gave me. Wale's tone was brisk as he spoke over the phone.

"Before he resigned, Dr. Olaoye informed the Dean that the stories had destroyed his social and family life. He pointedly accused the Dean of fabricating the rumours as an attempt to ruin him. This, of course is absurd. But a number of people seem to believe in the authenticity of the story and they repeat it everywhere. I don't think it is any personal malice for Dr. Olaoye, though—probably just idleness. Or maybe what the Germans call *Schadenfreude*. Meanwhile, the faculty is now trying to do a hush job."

Two months after the Dr. Olaoye incident, I was at home on holiday and Simbo was visiting. She was a plump and cheery girl with a practical head on her shoulders. We sat in the living room. Although the television was on, we were more interested in our cozy chat. Having traversed a variety of topics, we eventually got to the Dr. Olaoye fiasco. I related again my fruitless search for the origin of the damaging rumour.

"You know that day that Dr. Olaoye tried to have a go at you?" Simbo asked suddenly, as if remembering something. "Do you recall telling me about his attempt at Moremi cafeteria later that night?"

"Yeah, sure," I said, wondering where she was taking the conversation.

"Remember your exact words? You said 'The man just bent over me, right there, with the door open, anybody could have walked in' and I laughed and replied 'Imagine, it could have been the Dean that entered and caught you guys'."

I struggled to recollect my words. She was right, but I was still confused. "So, what has that got to do with anything?"

"Well, I've been thinking of this for a while. There's this funny theory in physics that suggests that it's the act of observing an event that forces the direction that event takes or something like that. You know? So, if you have no interest in an event, nothing would have happened. But by looking for something to happen—something actually does happen. It's a strange idea, really and I've been musing on how this could apply in this Dr. Olaoye business. You should look it up if you have the time. It's an interesting aspect of quantum physics."

"Go on with your gist, Simbo," I shifted in my seat, uninterested in her academic distractions.

"Well, do you remember the girl who was seated behind us at the cafeteria, that Bose—the short one? I think she must have heard us, maybe partially. I've been thinking she must have distorted what you said that night, and told a different story to someone else, until it took the proportions it eventually did. It's crazy, I know. But Bose is a slut and she has a penchant for such stories."

Stuck In A Box

My gal is in town, and I'm stuck in a box.
She came downtown for some cuddles and some talks,
I promised her a weekend, ice cream, and some fun,
But Saturday morning, the boss calls me on the 'phone;
"Get to the office, this weekend's no vacation."
I try to explain, "Sir, I have an obligation!"
His angry voice down the line is plain and real,
So, it's down to the office and goodbye to my gal.
I'm stuck in a box, I'm stuck in a box,
I see it around me, it's my life and it sucks.

There's a party, Tuesday night, for boys in the town,
Been no reunion since we doffed the stuffy grad gown.
I was tipped to be MC for my carousal and jokes,
I practised on my jigs; to get a laugh for the folks.
Party was on the mainland, 8 o' clock on the dot
But the boss man he comes, hands me a new report.
"See that you handle this before you leave for home."
I stared at the ream, and I thought, this is doom!
I'm stuck in a box, I'm stuck in a box,
I see it around me, it's my life and it sucks.

Told my old people I'll be home for the hols,
All they've had of me are the little phone calls.
My life is a box; I've tried hard to explain,
The excuse has grown weary; and they no longer
    complain.
So, its home for the *hols*, I'll be down for Christmas.
We'll sit down by the tree, catch up and converse.
But the Big Boss he shows again with a grin and
    a sneer,
"Sorry to disappoint," he says "we have no
    Christmas here!"
I'm stuck in a box, I'm stuck in a box,
I see it around me, it's my life and it sucks.

SEVEN:

The Sum of His Power

Whenever Richard Cory went down town,
We people on the pavement looked at him:
He was a gentleman from sole to crown,
Clean favoured, and imperially slim.

EDWIN ARLINGTON ROBINSON, RICHARD CORY

On a rainy morning in June, two men woke up on their separate beds and began the set of routines that would usher in the day as they set out to earn a livelihood. In their different locations in space, both men listened to the sound of the rain. They both approved of the weather, but from different perspectives — one of the men interpreted the rain as a symbol of divine blessing, the other regarded it as a drab and dismal downpour.

As he woke up in his bed without enthusiasm, Segun Sosanya came to a resolute conclusion that life in general, and his life in particular, was not worth living. He was 26 years old, a bright and talented lawyer working his way up at a high priced Broad Street firm. He lived in a suburban neighbourhood in Surulere, Lagos, and by the general accounts of his peers and superiors, he was a bright young man destined for an even brighter future.

79

However, on this overcast morning, his thoughts were a dismal reflection of the stormy clouds gathering over the Lagos metropolis. His mind spiralled and twisted in anguish as he sought a redefinition of his existence. His physical self was calm, as always, and as he went through his morning motions, a casual observer would think him a cheerful person indeed.

Lines from Wole Soyinka's *Opera Wonyosi* beat a rhythmic refrain in his thoughts as he kitted himself up for work, as though the words were trying to create a sense of order to his agonised thoughts: *What is a man but the sum of his power, to kill or to spare and make the world cower, what is a man but the sum of his power to kill or to spare and make the world cower, what-is-a-man-but-the-sum-of his-power-what-is-a-man-but-the-sum-of-his-power...*

The sum of his power. Segun reflected on the phrase, checking the words in his mind, to decipher the sense they conveyed. A speech from a distant memory surfaced in his thoughts and seemed to build a lectern in his head: *Power is the measure of man's will. Man's will is determined by his purpose and a man's purpose defines his existence. An existence without meaning or purpose is but a lost echo in a distant mountain, a tale told by a fool, useless to self and anyone else. Man was cultivated for a purpose, and the will and power to pursue it.*

As Segun stepped out of his house that morning, he shivered as he reached the conclusion that his purpose in life was being thwarted steadily by events around him. Like mocking waves washing over the sand kingdoms of a helpless child, life was constraining him from all angles, gently but firmly pressing on him and erasing again and again every attempt he made to create order out of each chaotic wave.

Chief Daniel Olujide, SAN, Ph. D., and several other titles acquired in his fifty years on earth had never felt as full of life and vigour as he felt driving his Land Cruiser Prado from his Bourdillon residence towards Onikan. The chieftaincy title recently bestowed on him by the supreme ruler of the Egba people in Abeokuta was testament to a life of hard work deserving of compensation. His commercial law firm on Broad Street, Olujide & Co., was considered one of the finest in Lagos and was highly recommended by foreign and local enterprises. His law firm was the proud culmination of his lifework. As he drove to the office, flowing easily with the morning traffic, he silently mused on the clearly charted course that was his life. He started to reminisce just as some lines beat an inaudible tune in his head, somehow harmonising rhythmically with the car's movement. Lines from a favourite poem from college literature classes.

Whenever Richard Cory went down town,
We people on the pavement looked at him

He had graduated top of his bachelors' class at Oxford in 1977 and had continued on a path of academic excellence until he arrived, with a doctorate degree in hand, before the glass doors of the top New York law firm of Slate, Shriver and Dean in 1986. There he immersed himself in the legal world of corporate finance. His analytical mind was quick to pick up the nuances of high finance and capitalism, and in 1991 he kissed his white girlfriend a long goodbye and flew back to Nigeria, ready to set up shop in the economically open Lagos of General Ibrahim Babangida's regime.

The unexpected political and economic crisis of the mid '90s did not deter his ambitions, and while many law firms across Lagos were folding up, he followed the principle of six degrees of separation, reaching out to old schoolmates established in the mushroom banks across the country and offering to take on their litigation portfolios at little or no cost. Those were years of gruelling nights and little money. They were days of austerity when he had to mortgage the plots of land he had inherited from his father to the same banks he serviced, almost free of charge, in order to pay for the running cost of his small firm.

But his perseverance eventually paid off. The return to democratic rule in 1999 and the influx of foreign investment into the country meant he could once again take up corporate finance and leave the dank rooms of litigation to his associate lawyers. Then, like a boon from God meant specifically for him, the Central Bank of Nigeria began a consolidation programme which transformed his old clients from tottering savings houses into major financial institutions, and overnight, Daniel found himself the legal consultant to several international banking institutions.

And he was rich – yes, richer than a king–
And admirably schooled in every grace

With great clients came great wealth and even greater clients— and nothing succeeded like success. The years spent in litigation ensured that he soon attained the rank of SAN and was enlisted into the league of worthy personages in legal circles. He moved his firm from the living room of his Sabo home to three floors and a penthouse on Broad Street. His investments were as astute as his legal arguments, and he soon began to sit on the board of several blue chip companies, raking in dividends in cash and kind. To celebrate the firm's twentieth year, he and the two partners he had groomed over the years had rewarded themselves with a couple of cars each. With a beautiful wife who had retained her youthful elegance even after two wonderful children – one in the medical and the other in the legal profession – Daniel Olujide had nothing to complain about.

In fine, we thought that he was everything
To make us wish that we were in his place

Except the staff of his law firm.

Daniel's outlook on capitalism was utility-based. He was entitled to derive maximum satisfaction possible from money spent on his business, and despite the official ten hours his employees spent in the office, he was not convinced that he had obtained from them the level of input equivalent to the sums he paid in wages and salaries.

This discrepancy worried him at night, and his testy reply to his wife's amused questioning was that he was entitled to obtain everything life owed him.

To give him more peaceful nights, he ordered that closed-circuit cameras be installed at strategic locations within the premises of his law firm to monitor employee activities. In the evenings, he watched the recorded scenes for hours—reviewing and analysing his employees' input while mathematically calculating what he expected them to be producing against their actual work output.

Predictably, his employees were always in the red—they owed him hours of time.

Although Daniel was not a cruel man, he believed in principles of efficient usage—a belief that sometimes resulted in, seemingly, cruel actions. To generate maximum efficiency, he prompted his employees to take desk lunches, implemented a new salary deduction policy for unaccounted work hours, specified bathroom break periods and ensured that internet access was restricted, making it impossible for employees to undertake personal activity on the internet while in the office.

But still, these measures did not give him the satisfaction he sought. Instead, he would often walk through the three floors of the firm with the conviction that once he turned his back on them, his seemingly busy employees would resume their nonchalant laughter and idle chatter.

As he manoeuvred the car from around Tafawa Balewa Square Junction into Broad Street, he concluded that there had to be a more effective way to derive maximum productivity from his employees—and he would find it. After all, the first purpose of law was to create order. Out of order emerged society, and out of society came efficiency. He was a *damn* good lawyer and no problem was too complicated for him to resolve.

Although he had no conscious desire to end his life, Segun found himself contemplating the most effective form of suicide and as he walked down Broad Street towards the building that housed the law firm of Olujide and Co. He concluded that jumping from a building would be horrendous and hanging unthinkable, but a lethal chemical dosage would be a fitting termination.

He thought of the psychological consequences of his death: the world forgives and even admires suicide only when it's by a celebrity; otherwise, you should have *fucked up* so badly that the sanest and most heroic thing you could do was getting rid of yourself. His "born again" parents would attribute it to a demonic possession — and he laughed at the idea. It is the work of Satan, they would conclude, for the devil is the sum of all illogic. His ex-girlfriend would act grieved for a while, but care less in the long run. Her hypocritical mind would point an accusing finger at herself for a total of sixty seconds before she would dismiss her guilt airily. After all, she was bound to reason; it had been a month since he walked in on her in passionate embrace with his best friend. A classic cliché. Their lust had cost him a lifelong confidante and a romance he had nurtured for two years.

He thought of his friends who would mourn him for a week and then continue with their lives without further thought. *Without further thought.* He thought of his co-workers and his work at Olujide and Co. and he frowned. The mindless, routine-filled, cubicle-partitioned, ant colony job that allowed him to eat well, dress well, sleep well and live — poorly. His work made him miserable, he had long realised.

Parents were not a life choice — the best way to deal with antagonistic parents is to ignore them. And ignore them he did. *Romance was replaceable and another friend could always be found. But productivity lost meant an existence terminated.* It was his work that made him miserable. He no longer felt productive, and yet he had no will to find a new purpose in life. His existence was unjustifiable to any living thing, and at his workplace he felt even more useless with every pressing weight of his employer's unending restrictions. But death would be a cure for him. *Death is natural. A man dies, another is born. Nothing is good, nothing is bad, and life is merely a cycle. And even empty space has energy—or so the scientists say.*

And what about the law he had studied and practised for the better part of his self-conscious life? The law was merely a part of society, nothing more. And despite the misguided admiration of lawyers from which he had benefited over the years, he found no satisfaction in the profession. He had since concluded that most of his fellow lawyers were pedantic not logical; confusing academic arguments for intellectual discourse and blindly following precedence instead of a philosophical approach.

But what makes a man philosophical?

Segun sighed as he thought about the question. What makes a man philosophical? Was it the ability to elucidate philosophical thoughts? No, that couldn't be it. Maybe when an individual is able to explain *why* he or she does or omits to do something, and can relate that action or omission to a personal principle, and then relate that personal principle to the general existence of humanity—only then can such a person be called philosophical.

He considered the thought in his mind, running a mental quality assurance test; seeking to fault his own answer. But he knew he was running from the underlying issue that bothered him. He knew his problem: he had no answer to the question *why*.

As he trudged the road, he sighed, knowing he could not take the first step to being considered philosophical. He could not explain why he woke up every day and went to work. His life had become mechanical, meaningless. He was caged in, and what he wanted was freedom from the black box that bound him. What he desired was power, the ability to say: *fuck this shit*, and put an end to it all.

The Senior Advocate of Nigeria enjoyed the smooth feel of his new car as he switched gears and stepped on the gas, speeding along Broad Street. He admired the orderly precision and logic behind the movement of his hands and feet and the instant response of the car. This was how things were meant to operate—life, family, business, institutions, society—on a principle of response to logical instructions. Efficiency. Turn the wheel, change the gear, and cue satisfactory reaction.

The young lawyer, his mind overshadowed by turmoil and his thoughts gradually dispossessed of logic, crossed the wet road of Broad Street in a blind daze—his physical reflexes oblivious to the free flow of the Lagos Island traffic. His psyche had summed up the totality of his life and found it without meaning and purpose, and so he was heedless of the traffic lights halting pedestrian movement and powerless before the ominous roar of the Land Cruiser flying down the road.

Daniel's first perception that something was going horribly, horribly wrong arose in a panicked flurry as his feet seemed to freeze while attempting to push down the car brakes.

How not to kill, how to spare?

In a brief vision, Daniel saw the logical consequences of the current event: the police interrogations, the ensuing scandal, the anxious clients, the ravenous rival law firms, everything he had built up in five decades: overwhelmed and redirected in a second's involuntary action.

How not to kill! How to spare!

But at this moment, Daniel's mechanical power over life and death was futile. His car smashed into his employee at seventy kilometres of speed and steel, and then rode over the body, dragging it a few metres further, sharply closing the book of the young man's life and redefining, in a dark and terrible way, the sum of his power.

The Way The World Began

Woman was made of bone
 And man was made from clay
That's the way the world began
 And the way it's still today

I worried over a pretty girl
 Hoping one day I'll tell her my mind
Then having told, I worried more;
 All she did was leave me behind

An axiom I once came across
 States: if you don't know the genesis
Don't be carried by the exodus
 Yet, this I failed to keep in view

Having learned the truth of these words
 I hardened me, a will of steel;
Duly ignoring those I most pined for
 Bringing all emotions to a heel

Who'd have guessed that time alone
  Would make me more appealing
To those who then had scorned my own,
  And left me for a weakling?

Yet, now I'm wedded and bedded
  I still feel a tiny gnawing
Wondering if I really haven't lost
  To those who called me weakling

'Cos 'woman was made of bone
  And man was made from clay
That's the way the world began
  And the way it's still today'

EIGHT:
Sticks and Stones May Break My Bones

"My mother was a motherfucker, you know. She would flog you like a man. You know how? She'd say: 'Touch your toes. Bend down.' And it was batabatabatabatabata...!*"*

CARLOS MOORE, *FELA: THIS BITCH OF A LIFE.*

I am running hard now, jumping obstacles and turning corners. Fast, frantic and desperate—but easily. Running is my thing. I was made to run. My sweat also runs, sprinting from the roots of my dreadlocks and down to my face. Behind me, a thousand feet are also running, they are chasing after me. A thousand feet intent on inflicting, on me, the frustrations of their own lives. A thousand furious feet of outraged traders. They were looking for a scapegoat, and I had volunteered for the job.

Catch am! Catch am! Thief, thief, thief!

I am desperate but exhilarated. I enjoy the run. I can feel the press of the heaving mass behind me, like petrol fumes at a filling station— invisible but overpowering. The incensed market had gathered for a hunt and its attention is now on me. I am equally determined to outrun the market, and I had been doing fine.

Originally, I had been running without direction but now I was intent on getting to the billboard in the distance. It was a tall structure, and the display stood against the sky, advertising bathing soap. The fresh and inviting face of the girl in the advert motivated me to run faster. If I could get to the billboard, I could slip behind the confused garage of buses in the area underneath it and escape from the thousand feet swinging after me.

The sweat drops running on my face were beginning to blind me, but I do not dare to pause the rhythm of my moving arms and free my face from the distorted view. The billboard is the goal. I have to get to the billboard and I would score.

The billboard had been part of our conversation earlier in the day. I had been lounging at the market bus stop with my friend, Jigga. We'd made some good money by noon and we were happy to relax for a while. We were as drunk as empty beer bottles and feeling higher than birds. Whenever the market girls passed us, teasingly swaying their bodies while balancing baskets skilfully on their heads, daring us to drop all and come after them, we would promptly whistle an appropriate exclamation and thrust out our chests in mock courtship.

Our day had been typical. As soon as a commercial bus came to a halt at the bus stop, we would jump before it and harass the driver for our "commission" — as mandated by the transport union. Sometimes we met with resistance, sometimes we got cooperation. Jigga was the more physical of the two of us. He wouldn't hesitate to unhook a windscreen wiper from the bus of any difficult driver and dare the driver or conductor to fight him. He was built like a bulldozer, and he had the attitude of one — he didn't give a damn about anything. Wary drivers and conductors settled matters with him without much persuasion, but sometimes we came across opponents who were equally eager to exchange punches and so short, rapid fisticuff would begin. A blow or two, and the matter was settled—with Jigga usually getting the best better of the encounter. But mostly, we got cooperation. That was the everyday life of a market tout.

So, earlier in the day, Jigga and I had been comparing the physical traits of some girls who had just passed us.

"That Aisha fine, men. Her *yansh* just make me wonder." I joked.

"Yeah. Aisha fine. But she no fine reach Tutu. That one *na* correct African babe. The way she *dey waka*, men, my body just *dey* on fire."

"*Ah*, but *dem* no fine reach the Delta babe," I retorted promptly. "*Na* she fine pass."

"Which Delta babe?"

"See *am*." I pointed to the billboard looming across the road away from the market.

Something about market aesthetics seemed to dictate that girls must look ugly in the markets. The girls come to the market without dress up or make up. Even the beautiful ones we flirted with usually looked hustled and roughed up as they struggled to trade at best prices. Uncombed hair falling out of scarves, bra straps hanging askew, and trousers rolled at ankle length—the market was generally an ugly sight.

But the girl on the billboard was untouched by the market.

The perfectly crafted and flawless face of the girl in the soap advert looked out silkily from the billboard. The fair skin, the small, sweet lips, mildly forming a smile and the eyes that expressed the innocence of a child all combined to choke me every time I looked at the billboard. Her picture was a welcome contrast to the surrounding environment. She inspired in me a desire, a painful yearning for an ideal. She was the ultimate form of woman—and I was certain that somehow, someday, I would get to meet a girl as perfect as the one on the billboard.

"*Ah*," Jigga said, looking at the advert. "You know say na you go school, illiterate no dey look signboard. Yes, the a'vert girl fine.

Even *sef*, I sure say I *don* see her before, she enter one supermarket for the other side of market one time like that."

I was sceptical. There was nothing preventing a model from patronising a supermarket in the market, but the odds that Jigga had run into her were too high. I expressed my doubts.

"*Walahi,*" Jigga was adamant.

"*Abeg*, come, show me this supermarket *wey* you see the babe, *make I see am.*"

"You wan' see? *Oya*, let's go. In fact, we fit see the girl again *sef*"

Jigga was a joker, but I went along with him all the same. I was unable to resist the thought that the girl of my fantasies could have walked the same grounds that I walked. I went with Jigga, hoping, even though I was certain that I could as well have hoped to run into my mother as well as into the girl on the billboard.

I can see my mother's face now, sad as usual, eternally expressing her disappointment in me. I can see her watching me run from my pursuers, indifferent to my plight, convinced that I had brought it all upon myself. She had wanted me to have a professional career; a university lecturer at the very least, a lawyer at best. But I had wanted to be a football player. I still want to be a footballer. As far back as I can remember I'd always wanted to run on the soccer fields streaking shots into open goal posts. Growing up in a rural environment did not take away this ambition; there were many fields of green grass in my small town, witnesses to days of continuous play.

Jigga's statement earlier in the day was right; I was the educated one. My mother had ensured that. My father died before I was born, drowned in the river that flowed through the town. My mother never regained her sense of happiness after she got the news of his death.

Mostly left alone, I'd become an avid reader at an early age, reading the words and enjoying the stories that came my way, but never the ideas. I was uninterested in the ideas and the places the books opened up to me. But I loved the tales. In school, I was poor at figures but had a way with words; otherwise, I was apathetic to the schooling concept—although education was a different thing. I struggled through secondary school and my first year at the polytechnic before finally calling it quits and dropping out. The few friends I had were not supportive; they considered it a bad move, but I didn't care.

I cared, though, about my mother's reaction. She was furious.

"What do you mean you're not interested in school? Even if you want to play football, you need to be educated. Are you mad? Has someone bewitched you?"

Then she lapsed into a stream of lamentations all geared at the imaginary enemies trying to destroy her lifework and drive her insane. For several days she couldn't speak to me without her voice expressing bitterness.

Soon afterwards, having decided that there was nothing more I could do at home to help my ambitions, I left home, at the age of 17, trekked to the nearest interstate expressway, hitched a series of rides and made my way to Lagos.

The football academy I intended to sign up with was located in the heart of Lagos, and without hope of accommodation or a means of livelihood, I arrived in Lagos and began a new life. I tried to get a clerical job but the hours were discouraging. I would have no time for my football training. So, to pay my living expenses, I did odd jobs for people and manual labour—from construction sites to beer depots—encouraging myself with the thought of future fame and glory. I was certain that the day would come when the people I laboured with would point me out as one of theirs.

I was ready to pay my dues and I got to pay them. It was a tough life.

Several nights I would lie awake on a thin mattress inside the small room I had rented, awake with despair, feeling the hopelessness of things and tempted to drop everything I was doing in Lagos and run back home, curl up in the comfort of my mother's house and experience a little sanity.

Night after night, I would lie on my thin mattress and think of my mother. I realised I had not been fair to her—despite her flaws and her stubborn determination to control my future—she always wanted the best for me. But these sentimental thoughts always faded with the dawn. In the mornings, I was determined not to go back until I had something to show for my flight. I was certain that the best act I could do for my mother was to come back home only when I was successful. Anytime earlier would seal the disappointment that she had come to have in me.

I met Jigga after playing in a football match at the local sports centre. He had hailed my skills after the match and I had been flattered. He liked soccer as much as I did, though he was not a player. He was curious about me, constantly wondering why I was not aspiring to a white-collar job. He was illiterate and could only manage to read a few common English phrases and was consequently respectful of my knowledge. We became good friends—an odd pair.

His daytime job was as an *agbero* in the local market park. But at night, he wheeled out his *okada* and ran it around town, after the legal hours for commercial motorbikes. According to him, the risk of being stopped by the police for transporting passengers after the legal hours was minimal compared to the returns he derived from the literal moonlighting. Besides, all he had to do, if stopped, was bribe the police and be off on his way. He was right. On the average, he made more money from his nightly forays than the daytime motorbike riders, and he incurred fewer expenses too.

Shortly after we became good friends, he invited me to move in with him and share the rent. I accepted eagerly and soon settled into an easy routine: I went for my trainings, did the odd job and assisted Jigga in the market park to supplement my earnings. I had done similar work before, it was nothing new: life is a cycle, like they say—until you hit a billion dollars. Then it becomes a straight line.

Two events happened that seemed to be directed by some callous fate at stalling the progress of my life. The first was the break in my training programme. Almost two years after I came to Lagos, and about eight months after I registered at the football academy, it was closed down. The manager had been defrauding the company, we were told. And that was it. No refunds, no referrals.

I was worried about my next move. I was not well known to local clubs to be signed up professionally and I could not afford the fees of the other academies in town.

"*Wetin* I go come do now?" I asked Jigga.

"Relax," Jigga said dismissively, "I go find person *wey* go help you."

He planned to approach one of the motor-park godfathers for assistance, but he wanted me to show commitment by working as a garage tout for a while. Like every other not-so-legal business, members of the inner circle were wary of strangers. I didn't mind the wait. At that point I was ready to take any offer that would help my plans.

Then my mother died—the second event. I got the news through a messenger. There was nothing I could have done, or could do. Her family, who considered me more a stranger than a relative, had buried her. What little property she had was already taken up by her sisters. I no longer had a home to go back to. When I got the message, I laughed hard as though it was an elaborate cosmic joke. The type of laughter that was meant to disguise my fear of the truthfulness of the news.

It wasn't a joke. I took a bus to the hometown and confirmed it. My mother's grave was ordinary and apathetic. She was forty-one. Her death certificate said she died from diabetes but I knew it was from heartbreak. I had nothing of hers to keep as a relic, not even a picture. I went back to Lagos, listless.

⚜

I saw the figurine sitting in a shelf labelled "AFRICAN ART" and I totally forgot our motivation for being in the supermarket.

Jigga and I had made our way to the store where he claimed to have seen the girl on the billboard. The day was young, and with our jeans and t-shirts we could pass for a pair of hip students, so we entered the store just for the pleasure of sightseeing. It was then that I caught sight of the figurine. Polished wood, it depicted a nude woman balancing a tray on her head while she knelt in ritual posture. It was a common carving. However, the slight chip on the black base of the wood held me in shock. It was impossible that two similar carvings could have the same chipped off base.

I had toyed with my mother's wood figurines as a child; she had a collection of these little carvings, displayed on her dressing table, a gift from her mother who in turn had received them from my great grandfather, a traditional carver. They depicted women in different postures and handling different objects. More importantly, the figure of the woman with the tray on her head had a chipped off portion on the wooden base from some forgotten accident. I was as familiar with these wooden figures as though they were childhood friends. I was certain that the kneeling woman with the tray had once been part of the collection that belonged to my mother.

I don't believe in signs and I had long stopped being superstitious. A rough life didn't allow for fancy beliefs. But as I looked at the carving on the display shelf, I was certain I had been given a sign. Having the figurine would give me a new connection to my mother—and I desperately needed that connection. The carving was a second chance to retain my mother's essence within my life. A deep hunger seized me. More than anything else, I wanted to recover the figurine, possess it and take it to a place where I could see it every day and have it all to myself. This was all I had left of my mother.

Without much thought about the implications of the act, I grabbed the figurine impulsively and ran out of the store as fast as a goalkeeper who suddenly realises he had strayed too far into the field. I thought I heard Jigga call out my name in wonder, but I was too excited to care.

But I was unlucky, one of the guards outside the store was anxious to enliven his day. He had cried out: Thief! The market heard—and had taken up—the cry.

And now, I am quite close to the billboard, this chase is almost over. I can still feel the pressing weight of the market, but their shouts are futile. Some of them do not even know what I am being pursued for, but they pursue all the same. I run even faster. They may not know it, but they have a footballer to compete against.

Hold am, catch am, thief, thief, thief!

But what have I stolen?

Something hits me hard. I flinch and nearly lose my balance; I did not think my predators would get violent so suddenly. This is mad. Something else hits me in the shoulder. A wincing pain goes through me. I get frightened. Some crazier people must have joined the chase. This was no longer a joke. I should stop and explain to them that it was a mere carving that belonged to my mother. It was nothing to get worked up about.

A loud bell goes off in my skull and there's an irritating ringing in my ears. I see that I'm on the floor, I must have been stunned. Something had hit me on the head. I open my eyes and see that the crowd is on me now. They are excited and murderous. I am getting kicked and taunted. Occasionally, someone would move close enough to pull my hair and then dash back into the safety of the crowd.

Thief, thief, thief!

My mouth forms words of protest at the punishment, nobody hears me, nobody is listening. But I have not stolen anything, I think. This has been a misunderstanding. I am sure if I were given a chance to explain myself, this would be sorted out. The crowd does not seem interested in my side of the story. The bloodlust that possesses the crowd is as visible as a distinct presence. I can't make out faces, just monstrous shapes. My body seems to have become numb to the pain travelling through my nerves and the crowd around me fades into nothingness as I stare up into the sky.

The girl on the billboard is smiling at me, her face is gentle and caring, a stark contrast to the face of my mother that I had been trying to please. The girl is not demanding any sacrifice from me; she doesn't look disappointed that I missed the shot, that I couldn't score the goal even though the net was wide open, that I am now on the market floor, getting my face kicked in. I smile at the thought of her perfection and let go of the carving in my hand.

I am aware that someone is pouring petrol over me but everything is alright.

An Epistle

Yesternight,
I woke up in the dark
Thinking,
A sober mien on my visage
And

My voiceless thoughts
Spiralled and twirled
All around you
And

I wished you were here
By me,
You, my divine sin,
My saving fault

I pulled the coverlet
Around me and saw you
Glimmering in silk and satin
The rainbow, woven in your hair

And your graceful smile
Lulled me
Back into a peaceful
Fantasy.

♡

NINE:

The Bludgeonings of Chance

In the fell clutch of circumstance
I have not winced nor cried aloud
Under the bludgeonings of chance
My head is bloody but unbowed.

W.E. HENLEY, INVICTUS

I watched quietly as my wife's coffin was lowered into her grave. The clergyman was intoning the usual formulas. Our friends and family stood around me under the Lagos noonday sun, with someone occasionally breaking into loud sobs. My wife had been killed in a freak accident, dead because a gully in the Benin-Ore Expressway had surprised her in the night as she journeyed towards Lagos. Her car had flown off the road; she had not survived the shattering impact.

The atmosphere was depressing enough. The overcast daylight, the litany of the priest and the mournful wailing of the gathering all contributed to my depression. To escape the madness that seemed desperate to break out from within me, I tuned out the words of the preacher and let my mind wander into reflection.

The puzzle of death is in its finality, I thought. *In this puzzle lies the ache, the sorrow, the bitterness, and the fear.*

But everything that happens in life has to have a reason. Or isn't that what people say? Maybe after death, we get a chance to examine if and whether all the brushstrokes of our lives, big and little, are tied into one overall pattern, one sensible picture. Will we be given the opportunity to examine the causes and effects of what seemed like completely random events?

I remember trying to scale the broken-bottle studded wall of our compound as a kid, so I could retrieve a football that had fallen in the abandoned building next to us. I was an expert at climbing—several mango trees in the suburbs of Abeokuta could testify to my nimbleness. I scaled the fence and got the ball. However, climbing back into our compound, I missed a footing, and the result was a deep gash on my chin and a few stitches after the trip to the clinic. I got reprimanded, and I got some sympathy. There was no other outcome, the scar has long disappeared, and the memory, virtually erased. There seems to be no real purpose to the event. It certainly was not just the pain, I had felt pain before then, and even more pain afterwards. It was definitely not the lesson my parents drew on my behalf; not to scale walls, I scaled the same wall and many others afterwards.

Existentialism is a depressing philosophy.

But I was forced to be existential as I watched my wife's lifeless face, serene in its silk lined coffin. I could think of happier times and days, when we both ran wild and carefree, blissfully unaware of death's proximity. Now, I am the surviving actor in the last act of our joint drama, and when the gravediggers throw the final spade of grit over her grave, the story of our lives would have come to a complete circle.

♡

Three years ago, I was 26 years old and I had just finished serving the country in the youth service scheme. After the service year, I had decided to go into business instead of seeking employment. A number of people prefer that family, friends, society and chance dictate their careers, material aspirations and other pursuits. I do not consider myself one of those people. I have always acted on the basis that my life was mine to control. With that philosophy in mind, I had filed away my school certificates, and had become self-employed.

Opportunities abound in Lagos for a young person with the right mixture of patience and ambition. I worked with a friend in establishing a media and advertising agency in Lagos, and in six months, business was booming. By contemporary standards, we were doing fine, we had four graduates as employees, a prime commercial district office space in Ikeja, Lagos and a car for the firm—the money for all these was derived from the capital we put up and the profits of a quick job that came in just as soon as we started.

This was the period when the 21st century global economic crisis was at its hardest, and major companies were spending more than usual on their corporate image. Public relations had become very important and customers and clients had to be reassured of business stability. It was a season for media agents and my partner and I were quick to cash in on the panic wave. *"By their ads you shall know them"* was our motto, and like I said, we were doing fine.

Except for one thing. There was hardly any physical cash in our pockets. We had the partnership profits, of course, in the bank. We had the expense account—for overhead costs, staff salaries, and production costs. But, as partners, we could only wait for the next profitable venture before having any substantial personal money. All I had was a day-to-day expense allowance of one thousand, five hundred naira. I had my personal investments, and I had some five thousand naira in the bank—for emergencies.

So, I lived with the financial knowledge that I was working for more money. I cheerfully spent my expense allowance and carefully planned my long-term investments. The future was stretched out for me, I had a business, I had no boss, and I enjoyed my work. Nothing was left to chance, and nothing could go awry without being remediable.

One week, a new deal came in for us. It was a simple job—we were to design a brand logo and stationery for a new client. After our staff finalised the design of the documents, I sent it through email to our printers for a test print. The printers delayed in sending the prints to me for two days, nonchalantly excusing themselves until, frustrated, I called one of their workers, an acquaintance of mine to bring them to me personally. He agreed to do this only after I promised to pay for his transportation.

After the call to the printers, I realised I had just one thousand naira on me. It was a Friday, my partner was out of town and so I could not write a cheque to withdraw more funds. I decided that I would give the printing staff the money on me and withdraw my emergency funds from the bank on my way home. I needed money for the weekend.

As planned, the printing staff came and left—with my money. After closing the office for the day, I walked down to the street with the nearest bank. At the ATM, I waited in queue for my turn at the machine. I slotted in my card and first checked my balance: ₦5,610. The message on the screen asked: *Do you want to perform another transaction?* I confirmed a withdrawal of five thousand naira and then waited for the machine to whirr and produce the naira notes from the slot. I hoped they would be clean notes. The machine whirred and nothing happened. Leisurely, I repeated the process. This time, however, the message that stared back at me from the screen was alarming: *Insufficient funds*. Confused, I checked my balance again: ₦610.

I had heard of such glitches: the machine would deduct the requested amount from the electronic account without dispensing the cash. I knew I would get my money back by Monday. But this was the *worst* time possible to face a cash shortage: I was a victim of Murphy's Law. I left the ATM worriedly. I checked my jacket pockets and found an overlooked fifty-naira note. But, how was I to survive till Monday? I would have to get in touch with friends to deposit money in my account the next day at a bank that offered Saturday banking. This should solve the general financial problem; but for that evening, there were the specific and immediate problems of getting home, and eating a good dinner. I had fifty naira; ordinarily I needed a hundred naira for two motorbike rides home. But now, with my limited funds, I could take one motorbike, walk the remaining distance and then sleep that night on an empty stomach; or I could walk all the way home, strenuous but doable, and eat an unsatisfactory but sufficient fifty naira meal at night. I chose the latter.

So I started the long trek home. Never had a journey seemed so long, never had the streets been so alive with the aroma and whiff of fruits, fries, and food; never was roast maize so golden, and doughnuts so bronzed. My stomach rumbled in agony as I passed each loaded market stall. I felt the essence of poverty, hunger—stark, bloody hunger. I walked my lonely way from bus stop to bus stop and junction to junction. My jacket clung to my back, the fine tie on my neck now loosened, and my laptop bag slung across my shoulder as I kept jumping around avoiding the careless motorbikes. I felt foolish in my corporate costume as I trekked under the hot African sun. Fela's contemptible *Gentleman*.

The rumbling in my stomach got worse with every tired step. I was desperate to eat something, and I no longer cared about a proper dinner at home. Logic is a function of wellbeing—and a hungry man is never objective. I decided that if I was so broke, I might as well enjoy my last naira. I began to scan the street for what I could buy. Roasted maize! Of course! I stopped at the first seller's stand. Nothing on her stack was less than thirty naira. I contemplated the outcome of sacrificing my prized fifty naira for a cob of maize. I bargained desperately with the seller to sell me a cob for twenty naira but she refused and so I moved on dejectedly. Then I saw a seller who sold roasted coconut chips. I hurried forward. I bought forty naira's worth; the ten-naira change would go to the water seller who was just up ahead.

I stopped to buy the water. A girl was at the next stall arguing with a groundnut seller. She was wearing a yellow top with a multi-coloured drawing splashed over its front; a pair of blue jeans sat firmly on her while her nubile curves ran up to meet the beads skirting above the jeans. Fierce, dark sunglasses shaded her eyes and I waxed poetical as I appraised her:

A 'pox on your mores reforms
Here's to glorious female forms,
When a pretty waist steps in view
Rev up your praise and join the queue!

I sighed off my eyes and tried to get the water seller's attention, but from the corner of my eyes, I could still see the girl attempting to pay the groundnut seller with a one thousand naira note. I was going to ask for the sachet of water when I noticed that an argument had ensued between them. The girl had bought some groundnuts and had opened the packet before making payment for them. The groundnut seller had no change for the one thousand naira note, hence the argument. Apparently, a ten naira note would solve the problem, but she had nothing lesser than the thousand, and the groundnut seller was unwilling to let go. The two women had proceeded to argue on who had the responsibility for obtaining the change.

Impulsively, and rather out of character, I went over and gave her my, now beloved, ten naira note. She smiled, thanked me awkwardly, and I walked away. It was all very simple. I continued my journey home. Having walked on for some distance, I glanced back, saw her get into a car and drive off. Now I was going to have a dry throat till the next day.

But my wallet had fallen off my pocket after I withdrew the money for the girl. I did not realise this until I got home, and I suffered through an impecunious and dismal weekend. A poor man has nothing but philosophy, and I marvelled that despite my best attempts, fate still found a way to take a hand in my affairs. That weekend, I did my best to sidestep the effects of the uninvited actions, and continue with my life. But fate was not done. The groundnut trader had discovered, and held onto, the wallet until the next day when the girl passed. The girl collected the wallet from the trader and promised to get it across to me.

I was at work the next week, when she showed up in my little office like a returning vision. That was my wife—our marital future as then an unknown prospect. After the initial social wariness, typical between two strangers who pass along each other in the night, we had hit it off pretty well and became firm friends and, later on, lovers.

♡

I turn my thoughts back to the funeral. I am expected to throw the first fistful of dirt on the closed coffin, an impersonal black box, and I do this mechanically.

Fate had obtained another laugh at my expense. We had gotten married six months ago, and she was pregnant with our first child. She had discovered the pregnancy while on a journey, on a marketing tour for her business. She had called me over the phone from her hotel room.

"Hello darling, guess who's coming to stay with us," she teased.

"You know I dislike guesswork. Come on, just play nice."

She laughed. "What's so wrong with guessing anyway?"

"Well, for one thing, it shows lack of a plan. I'm not a gambler. I make decisions based on rational information only. Sorry, I can't guess, silly." I tried to convey my boredom to her with my tone to make her drop the teasing. "So, who are we having?"

"You dummy. Well, rationalise this: we're having a baby!" She laughed.

"We're having a baby?" My emotions were a whirl of excited thoughts. "Darling, this is exciting. Of course, you know you have to postpone this trip, dear. You have to come home right away!"

"There you go, planning things already. C'mon, I'm not done with the tour."

"Oh yes, you are. There's nothing wrong with planning. If our child is to have a solid future, we are going to plan things all the way to the end. Starting now." I was getting excited and I tried to calm down. "Please, just come home soon, okay?"

"Relax, dummy. I'll be in Lagos tomorrow." She had finally agreed.

She died along with our unborn child on the Benin-Ore road.

Now, standing by her grave, I laugh out loud at the cruel irony, startling my fellow mourners. I search myself for a lesson learned. Some silver lining underlying the unrelenting darkness of the horizon, a logical conclusion that would make sense of the twisted premises. *Two plus two should equal four. There has to be an answer to every question.* Otherwise, what was to be learnt in an unexplained event? That the interstate roads were bad or that death was depressing? I knew these facts already.

I laugh out loud again. This time, my brother-in-law comes over and takes my hand, murmuring something indistinct to the others before leading me away from the gravesite, far away into a distant place where fate's fickle fingers would be unable to pull apart the last strands of my dwindling sanity.

She's Waiting There For You

The traffic wriggles between us
Slithering from Ozumba to the Lagos Island
A growing snake, intent on devouring our day
I know exactly what's on your mind
As you dial my number and my phone begins to pulse:
It's going to be the same excuse I gave yesterday
Now I want to turn back, give up, so long
Then I hear the lines from that '80s song:
Gonna take a lot to take me away from you
Hurry boy, she's waiting there for you

The girl in pink beckons to me at the bar
She's the latest in a series of nightly fantasies
It's tempting to get up and follow her glowing siren
A sweet adventure in the shadows and crevices
Stolen kisses won't hurt you when you're far
My body desires, like an incontinent teen
But I remember your eyes, your lashes cast long
Sweeping like the lines of that '80s song:
Gonna take a lot to take me away from you
Hurry boy, she's waiting there for you

Sorry Tales

A minute ago, you called me on the phone
You'll soon be at my place, you're on the road
Happily, you tell me to prepare, you're not so far
I wonder at the source of the lightness in your tone
And my heart transforms into a heavy load—
You're calling me from another man's car
A stinging reply had come to my tongue
But it was stopped by that '80s song:
Gonna take a lot to take me away from you
Hurry boy, she's coming here for you

TEN:

When the Clouds Arrive

When the clouds arrive
We'll live on—Ocean Drive.

LIGHTHOUSE FAMILY, OCEAN DRIVE

The tragic event that would haunt me all my life began on a cold July evening several years ago. I was 18, a university sophomore and deeply infatuated with a female classmate. I call it infatuation now, but at that time I could have sworn it was love. I was at that age where everything seemed possible and teenage dreams were yet to be crushed by the realities of 21st century life. Looking back on those days when the fantasies of romance were the mainstay of college life, I shudder at the naïveté of youth.

Though I had scaled the hurdle of my first year and had rid myself of the stigma of being a freshman, I still lacked the ability to manage a coherent relationship with the opposite sex. I had a reputation as a budding politician–I was a representative in the students governing body–but I was unable to plead my cause before the girl I then believed I was in love with.

Her name was Rosemary and I had known her since our first year as classmates. I first saw her during the freshmen registration exercise. She was standing in queue, poised like a queen and affecting an air of nonchalance at the bustle around her. I was quick to assure myself it was love at my first sight.

I walked up past her, pretending to be interested in a notice on the wall. On my way back to my original position, I casually whispered a greeting.

"Hi," she replied politely and said nothing more. I had smiled sheepishly and walked away.

Before the end of the first semester, I had only managed to manufacture a couple of intelligible greetings—the total extent of our relationship. But by the middle of the second semester, my above average grades had created the opportunity for us to interact a little better. She had come to me for academic advice on certain classes she wasn't too happy about, and by the end of the second semester, our relationship had progressed to the exchange of genuine smiles whenever we passed each other on campus.

At the faculty dinner at the end of that first year, I had watched enviously as she danced with other guys in the room. But when the mix of crowd and music threw us together, and I finally got the chance to dance with her, I was too nervous to concentrate and I had tripped all over her feet.

"I'm really sorry!" I tried to shout to her above the din of the band. "I seem to have lost my dancing shoes!"

"It's okay," she said and we kept on dancing.

But the closeness of her body and the intimacy of the dance seemed to work against my reflexes and I kept stumbling around. Eventually, she smiled politely, whispered something inaudible, and left the floor gracefully while I shuffled off behind her, blaming myself for being a clod.

So, on the evening of the day that would haunt me forever, I was with a few of my male classmates, about five or six of us, sitting outside the faculty building and enjoying the breeze. We felt at peace with the world. Exams were still far and we were tossing yarns and analysing political trends in the self-assured way only sober young males—and drunken adult ones—know how to do.

Not long after we had settled into the evening, a sleek Mercedes Benz pulled into the car park and interrupted our chatter. Out of the car stepped Rosemary. I didn't require a degree in logic to realise that the man who drove the car, and patted her arm as she got out of the vehicle, was no relative of hers. I suddenly lost all interest in the conversation around me.

"Man, this girl *sha*. She too much," one of my friends commented in pidgin as Rosemary walked into the faculty building.

"Oh boy, forget *am*," another replied. "Her level pass your own."

"Which level? Person *wey* I enter *wella* for first year," said the first guy with a thinly veiled smirk. I looked at him in amazement. Mere mortals do not share beds with goddesses. And this fellow, despite his boastful assertion, hardly seemed worthy of my *Yemoja*.

"You did what?'" I asked with a frown.

"Sure, she's there for the taking, as long as you have something in exchange," the smug fellow replied. "Kunle and Tony here will confirm, and as for you, I'm sure she'll be willing to make out with you, at least, for the mere pleasure of it."

I looked at the other guys. *True talk*, they nodded in agreement. And as though to launch a fatal assault on my already shaken psyche, they went on to give me graphic descriptions of the sensual and material pursuits of the girl I idolised.

"But where have I been?" I asked, "I really like that girl, I mean, she's so—". I was unable to complete the thought and so the sentence lay broken.

"Listen man, sitting here moping will do you no good, if you want a piece of the action, just walk into that classroom and give her something in exchange." This advice was followed by a chorus of affirmations.

I wasn't as naïve as the boys would have me painted—at least, at that time, I didn't think I was. Instead, I have always considered it absurd that intellectuals—for so we considered ourselves—would seek to define a woman's character by her ability, or inability, to conceal her sexual appeal. Nevertheless, I had felt injured and I took the proffered advice. With wild fury coupled with a deep sense of the betrayal of my private affection, I left the gathering and went into the faculty building to seek her out.

She was seated in a corner in one of the classes, seated quietly in a corner, a book open in front of her. From the distance, she seemed lost in thought. My desire for justice spurred me on, knocking off my natural intimidation at her presence, and I went up and took a seat next to her. She glanced at me with a partial smile. And then I got a shock.

Her face manifested evidence of severe stress; my idealised image of her was a distinct departure from the reality that faced me. She looked strained, and a looming ugliness seeped from beneath her cosmetic-lined face. The lines on her face were furrowed, the caked powder highlighting the gaps. Strands of hair kept creeping out of the band over her head, and there were heavy bags under her eyes. From her reddened eyes and the damaged make-up, it was clear that she had been crying.

There and then, it occurred to me that once created, everything begins to wither, and the differences in aesthetic perspectives was merely superficial—inhabiting the time it takes to notice the depreciation of life.

Concerned about her state of health, I forgot the fiery wooing speech I had mentally rehearsed and instead asked how she was. She told me she was fine, smiled and turned to the open book before her. I watched her for a while. She appeared to have little concentration for the book. Her thoughts were visibly distant, her face: lost and confused. It bothered me. Gently, I told her I thought she needed to take a rest.

Then Rosemary told me her story, haltingly and sometimes, unvoiced.

"I'm in serious trouble. No I can't tell you what it is. Maybe you'll hear of it later." she started. "I know men. I know they mostly want me for my body. But, you are different, I know you like me, as I am—not for my body. I don't know why, but I know you like me. I wish you and I had been better friends. You're the only person I can talk to in that class."

And she went on in a disjointed manner, telling me her life story—a father who abandoned his wife for another woman, a mother who had to serve as a cook and waitress in her own sister's restaurant, the wayward brothers, her discovery of her feminine charms, how she put herself through school with her body—until she broke down crying, dejectedly looking at me for affirmation that she made the right choices.

A woman's body is hers, I told her. She is as capable of making her individual choices as any man—as long as she was able to handle the consequences of her actions.

"Really? You really think so?"

"Yes. Well, I suppose there should be a guiding principle for your actions—even if it's about money. But still, you own yourself, even if you are in a relationship with a man. The powers you give him over you are a privilege, not a right. Not *his* right—not even if he was your husband. Nobody has a right over you."

She sighed. Her voice was cracked as she asked me another question: "Do you know the Lighthouse Family song, *Ocean Drive?*"

"Yes." I nodded, wondering what that had to do with anything.

"It keeps playing in my head again and again. I love that song," she continued. "And right now, I need to be there, I want to go to Ocean Drive."

I puzzled over the meaning of her words, but did not ask for an explanation. She silently packed her books, and left me in the room, dazed; like the wedding guest in *The Ancient Mariner*, a sadder but wiser man.

A week later, I would re-examine our conversation and the cryptic words she left me with.

I had stood before my bedroom window watching a thunderstorm over the Lagos Lagoon and contemplated the news I had just received. The sky–*a crucifixion sky*, I had thought to myself–seemed to understand. The lagoon was a raging spirit, writhing as though tortured by the fierce whipping of the rain. In the distance was the vague outline of the Third Mainland Bridge, barely visible through the downpour. I thought of waves.

Ocean waves. Ocean Drive.

You can either know where a wave is, or know where it is going — but not both at the same time. I had known where Rosemary was; I had not known where she was going.

Her body had been found earlier that morning, bobbing on the edge of the lagoon. I had learnt the facts from one of her close friends. In an age and a country when a long-term infection with HIV was almost certainly fatal, it was with despair, but little surprise, that I took the news. She was dead and cold, but beautiful and untarnished, her suicide was a final act flung defiantly before an unforgiving Fate.

I called it a tragic event, I may be wrong.

Facebook Message to an Old Friend

Wish I could cross this cyberspace
and row over just to see your face
and try to see if you recall the days
of our infancy and we'll share the ways
we have tried to win this race
of life, and plenty more! (But face-
book is not physical) so I place
my thoughts in this line, which says:
"Have a splendid day! Wishing you good days
like this, and plenty more!" and healed our space.

ELEVEN:

The Black Box

"In the long run, we are all dead."

JOHN MAYNARD KEYNES

There is an element in humanity that makes a person confident and accepting when confronted with *certain* death. The ordinary ability of a rational human to survive a lifespan is a generic evidence of the existence of this element, for it is obvious to every self-conscious human being that he or she must die someday; yet, people go through life with an almost optimistic belief in the possibility of immortality. Without this element, without this mysterious optimism, men and women would instantly give up on life as soon as they became aware of the inevitability of death. Suicide is always an option, but it is generally considered an aberration—all men must die someday so why rush towards death?

These thoughts swirled in Egbuna's mind in a self-mocking fashion as he walked along the aisle towards the cockpit of the airplane. For almost an hour now, he had been confronted with the factual evidence of certain death and he was prepared for it. His mind, ordinarily rich in ideas, had, in these peculiar circumstances, begun to traverse space and time with even more whimsical notions.

When he boarded the plane in Abuja, his only thought had been to get to Lagos in time for a fine dinner and a good night's rest in his hotel room. He was looking forward to a meeting with the Lagos State Commissioner of Information the next day. Three months of pursuing a publication deal with the Lagos State Government had finally paid off, and the contract papers were ready for execution. His lawyers and his office staff had been on ground all week, shuttling between their hotel in Ikoyi and Alausa, preparing the papers. Egbuna's only role was to come to Lagos on Sunday, execute the documents early on Monday and be back in Abuja before the close of the business day.

In the last one hour, however, he had thought of the pending contract only fleetingly; instead his mind had dwelled on his children whom he would never see again and his wife with whom he had only a superficial relationship. He had not consciously thought of his children in almost eight years—not since the birth of his last child. But now he kept wondering about them, and about the kind of father he had been. His first child, Chris, a son with whom he had never had a convivial relationship, had recently graduated from medical school; his two daughters, Vanessa studying Business Administration in the university and Leander still in primary school. He kept trying to remember the age of his first daughter, but found it quite elusive. He remembered giving her money for her 21st birthday, but, right now, he couldn't quite place her current age.

His wife remembered everyone's age and birthdays; she was that kind of person. Sometimes it was a useful trait, but most times it was annoying. It was one of the little things that had driven a wedge into their relationship. Their arguments always grew from the most insignificant issues.

"Well, I always say you should stop being too possessive about the children. They are not exactly your property."

She would flare up at the remark from him. "Possessiveness is part of love. Parents should feel possessive about their children."

Ayo Ṣogunro

"Don't misunderstand me, Joyce. I'm not saying you should not love your children. But love is different from possessiveness. It's this kind of mistaken idea of possession that leads to murders. In fact, the more you love a person, the less you should hold a grip on them."

"Oh really? So I plan to murder the children, right?"

"That's not what I mean, Joyce. That's not what I mean at all."

When the pilot had announced, in an unbelievably calm tone of voice, the certainty of the plane crashing if it kept hovering for longer, and the improbability of all the passengers surviving, like a choreographed symphony, the passengers had gone through all the stages of grief—from denial to acceptance. Egbuna had watched his co-travellers with the cynicism of a man who had lost faith in his social construct—watching a drama performed by actors who had no idea they were acting out a script. First had been the rapid and spontaneous burst of spirituality of the people chanting "Jesus, Jesus," their ingrained spiritual invincibility preventing them from facing the reality of the moment as they denied the obvious, and then others, alternating between denial and anger, kept hurling insults at the crew and the airline: "I trusted you people!" a man had been shouting repeatedly from the back. "I trusted you people!" Others tried to be rational and kept looking for ways to help, asking the crew for what could be done to save the situation. The depressed were easily noticeable—a man had vomited and another seemed to have collapsed—even as the crew kept trying to reassure everyone.

Over the frantic cries and the prayers, the pilot had continued to speak. Though the plane was doomed and the chances of survival in the circumstances nil, all was not lost, he had said. Egbuna had listened to the pilot first with curiosity and then with growing hope— all was not lost—not yet. He had not been alone in this thought— because gradually, the noise in the aircraft had reduced and everyone had begun to come around to the stage Egbuna had started out with. Acceptance.

Death was an interesting idea. Just a month ago, he had escaped, with other people, an attempted bombing of the third mainland bridge in Lagos; but now, here he was on a doomed plane. Death had no timetable or date, people die simply because the opportunity to die shows up. The world spins around, and humanity merely turns with it, involuntarily. As Egbuna walked into the cockpit, the elusive memory came to him—she was still 21. His daughter was still 21! He remembered now that it was just over eight months since she celebrated her 21st birthday. He walked into the cockpit with the bounce of a man who had rediscovered life. He had a smile on his face.

"So exactly how does this black box work?"

The question was asked by one of the newspaper reporters surveying the disaster area. The charred remains of the fuselage of the crashed aircraft stuck out at an angle from the grim landscape like a leprous thumb. The morbid region had been cordoned off from the general public, but curious bystanders were at the fringes taking pictures with their mobile phones even though the sun had begun to set. The smell of charred flesh and rubber produced an unpleasant odour. The plane had crashed into a residential area and it was obvious that none of the passengers could have survived the crash. The black box in question had earlier been found and transported to the agency's office at the airport. But the agency officials and the reporters were still at the scene—investigating the wreckage.

The man to whom the question was posed hesitated a bit before answering. "Well, first, it's not exactly a *black* box; it's usually an orange coloured instrument, which should stand out from the wreckage of the plane."

"Really?" the reporter asked.

"Yeah. I don't know how to explain the details to you without sounding technical, but it's basically a recording device that records happenings on an airplane. Think of it as the survivor of the accident who tells you how it all happened. It's usually located in the cockpit and can record the flight data and voice data for up to 2 hours. Anything the pilot said up to the time of the crash should be captured."

"So we can use it to find out what exactly led to the crash?"

"Exactly."

The Director-General of the Aviation Authority was not happy. He sat in his office early on Monday morning and thought about the plane crash of the previous day. Already, the Minister of Aviation had called to find out what led to the plane crash. The Minister wanted information and he wanted it fast. The Director could not blame the Minister—the President was "on the Minister's case" and the Minister was passing the heat on to the agency. The Director had promised to give the Minister the relevant details as soon as the black box was decoded. But now, he realised he had promised too soon. Although the black box had been found and the information extracted, he had nothing to give the Minister—at least nothing of what he knew the Minister wanted to know.

How could the pilot of the plane have been so irresponsible? The Director thought bitterly. Not only had the pilot denied the agency an easy way of investigating the cause of the accident, he had also left behind a ton of unnecessary work for the agency to do. But again, the pilot had handled the situation with an understanding of human nature that had to be respected. Someone somewhere would definitely give him the appropriate recognition, but it wasn't going to be this Aviation Authority.

With a huge sigh, the Director wrote out a memo on what steps would have to be taken. Then he picked up his desk phone and dialed the Minister's number. When the call connected, he carefully explained to the Minister what they had discovered from the black box and what he thought should be done to salvage the looming political situation.

Joyce Egbuna stared at the slim envelope in her hand, recently delivered by a DHL courier, who had collected his delivery form and sped off away from her suburban home. It was from the Ministry of Aviation and she wondered what new information or condolence they wanted to give her. She went back into the house slowly and sat on her sofa. In the last one week she had reluctantly begun to come to terms with her husband's death. He was a good man who provided for his family, but he had also had a difficult relationship with her and the children. In deference to social norm, she tried not to think ill of him—but her husband had his faults. To her, the foremost of these was his disconnect from his nuclear family. He was a responsible man—but he extended his responsibilities only to the logical necessities, shying away from emotional understanding. She could not remember the last time they had a decent conversation and his children had grown up as strangers to him.

Now he was dead.

How would he view her, now alone without a husband? "When it comes to pure physical strength and stamina," he often said, "there is no male or female classification. Some people are strong; others are not. It is society that tells a woman to be 'prim and proper and delicate' not nature. A natural woman can be more fearsome than a man."

But Joyce had never considered herself "a natural woman". The idea had never made any sense to her during her arguments with her husband. Now, he was dead—and she felt she could understand what he had meant.

She opened the envelope. It contained a compact disc and a letter. The letter was brief: *"Dear Mrs. Egbuna, the Ministry of Aviation again sympathises with you over your recent loss. It is hoped that this message will help your bear your loss with fortitude. The enclosed CD contains an audio extract from the recovered black box of Flight 914. It contains a personal message from your husband to you. Our regards."*

The envelope dropped from Joyce's hands as she called her first son in a trembling voice. Chris came bounding down the stairs to his mother, paused to size up the situation and then collected the letter from his mother and read it. He took the disc and went over to the player. Mother and son listened as the electronic gadget brought to life the voice of their husband and father.

"Joyce. Our pilot has allowed those who wish so, to come up and leave a message for loved ones. I know I've not been the best husband or father and I hope you would take this message as a symbol of my remorse. Even though I will certainly not see you in this world again, please know that I die happy with the thought that I had one more chance to let you know how much I love you and the children. If there is a hereafter, I hope we would see each other there."

For Assange and Other Heroes

It's the strongest man who
Stands
When the rest of the world
Pleads
Bargains
Begs
Threatens;
Turn your back against the
Crashing waves
And watch in silent contempt
Those who being
Slaves from birth
Do not value
Rebellion;
It is for them to perish through
Ignorance
You shall continue to exist
Intelligently;
Wipe your dusty shoes
and depart their shores;
Truth
Was offered for free
But the lies found ready cash.

TWELVE:

The Wonderful Life of Senator Boniface

"The strongest man in the world
is he who stands most alone."

HENRIK IBSEN, AN ENEMY OF THE PEOPLE

*"The final party hosted by Senator Lawrence
Boniface will be remembered for decades to come.
For several weeks prior to the event, the Lagos
metropolis had been aglow with anticipation; the
media had publicised the event with aplomb and
the renovations in the Ikoyi palatial residence of
the Senator was a pointer to the seriousness of the
preparations. However, despite the public aura of
the event, attendance was strictly by invitation."*

FROM THE FRONT PAGE OF THE GUARDIAN NEWSPAPER

A party to be hosted by Senator Lawrence Boniface was nothing unusual in itself. Parties were a staple of the Lagos metropolitan high life. Weekday parties, morning parties, weekend parties, night parties, marriage parties, divorce parties, parties to celebrate death and parties to celebrate life, birthday parties and second birthday parties, housewarming parties, release-from-jail parties, thanksgiving parties, send-forth parties, welcome back parties, and of course, the absolutely-no-reason-for-the-celebration parties.

What was exciting in this case was the circumstance under which the good senator had decided to throw the party. Barely a month before the celebratory event, the senator had been a favourite for the Social Progress Party's presidential ticket in the general elections scheduled to hold in April. The SPP was the country's ruling party; its tentacles twined deep in twenty-seven out of the thirty-six states and firmly headquartered in the government house at the Federal Capital for over a decade.

It was with good reason that Senator Boniface was a favourite in the polls. Fifteen years before, at the age of thirty-nine, to the despair of his academic colleagues and the joy of the general society, he had quit his laudable career as a senior lecturer at the Sociology Department of the University of Lagos to take up politics full-time. Prior to his resignation, he was generally recognised as an outspoken critic of oppressive and inane government policies. He believed firmly in the duty of a government to take care of its citizens.

The force and aptitude of his suggestions had earned him, along with his lecturing duties, appointments as a Commissioner on several state and Federal Government bodies. Over the years, he had served on the Salaries, Incomes and Wages Commission; the Environmental Protection Agency; the Emergency Management Agency; the National Planning Commission; and the Consumer Protection Council. He transformed each body he served on from little-known government office blocks into virile organisations springing with usefulness.

In the political arena, Senator Boniface rode on his reputation as a social critic and government performer with the ferocity of a mad *okada* rider. His local constituency was quick to present him as their hero and voted him into the House of Representatives on the SPP platform. He spent his first term as a Representative cementing his political reputation. He never hesitated to sponsor bills that were beneficial to other geo-political zones besides his. And if a bill was not to his philosophical taste, he would staunchly oppose its passage. When coerced or cajoled to change his mind, he would defend his stance by referring back to his constituency: *My people must not hear that I voted for this law.*

During his second term as a Representative, he was appointed Speaker of the House. Having mastered the nuances of House politics, he was careful to maintain his personal philosophy of government responsibility but also learnt to compromise on lesser principles in order to secure favours. Though a public crusader against government corruption, he was quick to come to terms, privately, with the fact that he could not wipe corruption out of the legislative body he presided over. The House committees were clearly vehicles for promoting illegal wealth but as long as the wheeling and dealing was kept out of his sight, Senator Boniface also looked the other way.

After eight years as a Representative, he had accumulated enough public favour to risk running for the Senate, and he succeeded with a resounding victory. The country was astonished at the lack of opposition from his senatorial district. In fact, the opposition parties had proudly announced that he was their adopted candidate. The spokesman of the opposition's alliance was quoted as saying: "*We disagree with the Social Progress Party on many, if not most issues, but with regards to the candidacy of Lawrence Boniface, we are in full agreement. Only a suicidal person fights against a good thing.*"

From that period onwards, Senator Boniface became a political celebrity. With his good looks and the carriage of a movie star, the glamour media patronised him while the gossip columns serenaded their readers with innuendoes about his private life; his children and family were monitored and photographed and even advertising agencies approached him with suggestions for product placements and endorsements. Senator Boniface humoured the attention he received and regarded his celebrity status as a just outcome of his activities. His life philosophies had pointed to the conclusion that as long as he unwaveringly maintained the path he had chosen for himself, everything good would eventually come to him. With this optimism, he wholeheartedly embraced the attendant social and commercial benefits of his status. Within a reasonable period, he was able to purchase an extensive town house in Ikoyi and became known in his vicinity as a generous host and a fine party-maker.

Senator Boniface was not popular for his political philosophies; he was popular *in spite* of it. The bills he sponsored or promoted were not always passed—but that was only because the majority of his legislative colleagues were not as reformative as he was. However, he always did manage to raise political dust. As an overzealous television reporter once expressed, exaggeratedly, on national television: *In the words of The Hitchhiker's Guide to the Galaxy, Senator Boniface is more popular than The Celestial Homecare Omnibus, better selling than Fifty-Three More Things To Do In Zero Gravity, and more controversial than Oolon Colluphid's trilogy of philosophical blockbusters: Where God Went Wrong, Some More Of God's Greatest Mistakes, and Who Is This God Person Anyway?*

With Senator Boniface's popularity growing with each year, and the incumbent President in his second and final term, it was inevitable that the political pundits would point to him as a suitable candidate for the presidency. Television talk shows and newspaper columns featured the suitability of the senator's candidacy. A constitutional lawyer, during an interview, expressed the general feeling: *Boniface is just right for the job. Take it from any perspective: chronologically, he is not too young neither is he too old, he can adequately bridge the gap between the youths and the senior citizens; intellectually, I mean, here is an intelligent academic with a doctorate degree; experientially, his reforms, in the Environmental Protection Agency, for instance, has put a stop to the gas flaring issue; socially, he has a direct line to the mind of the man on the street and still manages to find favour with the top celebrities! What are we then saying? I have studied the political scenario for years and I can tell you with all due respect that this man is the best Nigeria has ever seen and will ever see!*

However, the leadership of the SPP was not as enthusiastic as constitutional lawyers. Senator Boniface was a good man, the inner caucus agreed, but he was difficult to contain. On several occasions, he had flouted party rules—for instance, attending promotional events sponsored by rival parties—and though he always had good reasons, his involvement was still embarrassing to the party. In any case, there was a hierarchy in place, and the proposed call for his nomination would upset the delicate structure of power. With this in mind, the Board of Trustees of SPP called a secret meeting of the inner caucus of the party. They had to settle the issue of Lawrence Boniface.

On the day of the meeting, Boniface sat before the elders of the party in silence as they chided him for listening to the flattery of ignorant people and putting himself on the queue of the duped. The meeting was in the form of a traditional village meeting—informal yet serious at the same time. It was held in the home of the Chairman of the Board of Trustees and in the midst of the pleasantries and dining, the senator's trial commenced.

They reproved him for his failure to silence the people who called for his candidacy and his apparent encouragement of the idea. *A wise man does not act on the music of praise singers*, they said. Afterwards, they assured him of the party's continued support of his senatorial post or if he preferred, a ministerial portfolio. *Just mention the office you want.* They rounded off the remonstrations by lauding his achievements and praising his dedication to the party.

The senator sat through all of these in silence and at the end thanked them for their patience with him. Then he went home and thought hard into the night. Though he had playfully mused about occupying the office of President in idle moments, he had never given it serious thought. If anything at all, he viewed it as a positive wave of public opinion merely consolidating his senatorial achievements. He had mentally waved aside the supplications and entreaties for his candidacy as the typical enamour of the African society with the man of the moment—here today and forgotten tomorrow.

However, the party had made a mistake in sitting him down and attempting to dictate the course of his life. As a party member, he was bound to obey the rules that ensured the coherence of the party, but not by any decision that would govern his values or threaten his personal integrity. If the party was going to determine who ran for the office of President solely on the basis of secret agendas, then he was going to disobey the party and run for the office of President.

But Senator Boniface was not a rash man; he had his staff conduct careful research and until he was convinced he stood a chance of winning the most votes, he kept quiet. Meanwhile, he set out on a subtle grassroots level campaign in a bid to improve his image as presidential material. He also reached out to groups outside the party to gauge their perception of the idea. It was a positive exercise. He became convinced that he would win a general election.

Party primaries, as simple as they may appear to an outsider, are a much more complicated process when compared to general elections, especially for a ruling political party. These primaries are usually more intense, more violent and even more demanding than the general elections. These features are inherent in the very nature of the primaries: several persons could run for an office on different political platforms, but only one could run as a party's candidate. The race to become a party's flag-bearer involved intense lobbying and politicking to secure the votes of the delegates. It was through the primaries that political parties showed their disregard for popular will, and many a good candidate had been felled by a bad primary.

The SPP was not exempt from these features, and as the primaries approached, the party's delegates became the most important persons within the party. Up to 500 delegates, elected or selected by a system of primaries and appointments from the local, state and federal levels of the party, would determine who was fit to run for the office of President. In most cases, these delegates were the true electorate; for in a strong political party, like the SPP, whoever they elected in the primaries would almost certainly go on to win the general elections.

The Party elders watched with increasing disapproval as Senator Boniface publicly announced his intention to run for the party's ticket and effectively posed a serious challenge to the candidate secretly sponsored by the party's inner caucus. The newspaper headlines ran wild with excitement; and around the country citizens tuned in on television to watch the opening of the senator's campaign. Unable to resist Senator Boniface in the face of popular goodwill, the godfathers of the SPP smiled into the camera lenses and granted interviews suggesting that it was their idea that *Boniface, our son*, contest the party's ticket all along.

The senator's campaign team set out to work on each of the delegates with an efficiency that would have made Sun Tzu proud. Delegates were zealously pursued around the country, wooed, cajoled and lobbied in every way possible—short of outright bribery. The delegates were encouraging in their responses: *Young man, you are preaching to the choir. I know Lawrence, he is a good man; be rest assured that he has my vote.* A firm handshake afterwards and the campaign team member would go away happily to report back that the nomination coast was getting clearer for the senator.

On the day of the primaries, the country watched with excitement. It was generally acknowledged that if Senator Boniface picked the SPP's ticket, he would definitely win the general elections. As if acknowledging that fact, opposition parties delayed their primaries and awaited the outcome of that of the SPP. The entire country focused on the SPP primaries and soon enough, the voting commenced.

After three hours of open ballot voting, the votes from each state were counted and announced. Senator Lawrence Boniface lost the primaries *without a single vote cast in his favour*. None of the delegates voted for him. For a moment, he was sure there had been an error until logic persuaded him that the absence of votes was not a mistake in counting but a cold, hard fact. The party had deliberately punished Senator Boniface for his stubbornness.

He stood up afterwards and acknowledged defeat. For a second time, he went back home and thought long and hard. The delegates had simply toed the party line without a care for moral values. They had sold the votes entrusted to them for political goodwill and had shown themselves for what they truly were—a cancerous decay in the flesh of society. He began to relive his interactions with the delegates before the primaries and with the thought of each reassuring smile, each hand grasp, each pat on the back that he had received, he felt unjustly deceived and bitter. He wept through that night over the rottenness of men.

Within a week, Senator Boniface had received offers from all the other political parties to run as their flag-bearer, but he rejected all the offers politely, yet firmly. He was a member of the SPP, and he was not going to change his party affiliations simply because he lost at the party's primaries. Privately, he also knew that running on another platform would not guarantee him a win. The SPP controlled the government and by extension, the electoral process. If they could make sure not one person out of over 500 delegates voted for him, rigging a general election would be much easier.

Instead, Senator Lawrence Boniface, loser of the SPP presidential primaries announced to a puzzled battery of pressmen that he had accepted defeat and in fact, had decided to throw a party in honour of the elected candidate as an indication of his willingness to accept the outcome of the primaries. The media went agog at the incredulity of the idea. Strong candidates who lost in the primaries were expected to quit the party; they did not celebrate the winners. The sentiments were dished out in approving clichés: *What a Senator! What a man! Gracious in defeat! Such a magnanimous individual!*

Senator Lawrence Boniface intended that his planned party would be remembered for decades to come. Accordingly, the senator personally oversaw every aspect of the event. After sending his wife and children on a vacation abroad, he had the house renovated and redecorated in SPP colours. His large living room was converted into a sizeable hall along with other rooms in the building to accommodate the guests. For several days, mysterious trucks trooped in and out of the compound, and to the eyes of an interested observer, apparently transporting construction equipment.

For the several weeks leading up to the day of the party, the Lagos metropolis was abuzz with anticipation. The news media shadowed the activities of the Senator, desperate to get more information; but despite the public enthusiasm about the party, attendance was *strictly by invitation.*

By noon on D-day, the guests started to arrive. The vehicles of the powerful and the wealthy dotted the senator's avenue with the elegance of a bridal parade, each new arrival flashier than the former. Either out of a sense of remorse or a failure to appreciate the irony of hospitality from a victim of their schemes, nearly all the party leaders and members of the inner caucus were present. The other guests included serving government officials as well as several influential political personalities. The Senator had selected his guests with extreme care — as he wrote in the personalised invitations sent to each of the guests: *This is a celebration in honour of the best among us. Your attendance is, without exaggeration, vital to the interests of the nation.*

The tables were set and the guests took their seats with the ease and attitude of people accustomed to the good life. The waiters were from the finest caterers and they ensured a steady supply of good wine and rich victuals. The conversations were easy and luxurious. Political differences were put aside and the joviality increased with every uncorked bottle of champagne. Party men and women bubbled with laughter and gaiety, cracking jokes, exchanging pleasantries and forging alliances as they raised toast after toast to the continued health of the good senator.

Sometime after the coastal sun had set, about two hours into the merriment, Senator Boniface went up to the small stage, a martini glass in hand, and asked for some silence as he had a few words to say in deference to the purpose of the celebration. He cleared his throat loudly to ensure full attention and began what he promised would be a short speech: *I thank you all for coming here today. Believe me when I say that your presence here is not accidental, every one of you here has been invited as an acknowledgement of your contributions to this great country. This is not to say others not here are irrelevant, but those of us here are the life and soul of our great party.*

The senator sipped from his glass and waited for the cheers to die down before continuing:

A few weeks ago when I lost the election, I was bitter for some time. But I realised that bitterness was not the answer to the questions raised in my mind by the primaries. After some serious mental exercise, I came to an absolute conclusion that the problems of this country could no longer be solved by ordinary political and social factors. Every one of us here is a testament to that conclusion. What do I mean? All of us present have achieved our positions of wealth and authority not by personal merit or popular will, but by making ourselves the stooges of political agendas.

By this time, the guests had begun to look at one another bemusedly, but the senator went on unabated, he had only just commenced his speech.

A number of us have sacrificed principle and conscience in order to attain wealth and power. Our corrupt political machinery has been so deeply entrenched into the society that it has now become difficult for the average person to emerge into the political limelight without being forced to submit to the self-appointed political godfathers.

I have led a wonderful life so far—my political occupation has been void of the influences of godfather masterminds, and I have paid the price for that omission by losing the presidential ticket of the SPP. But, forget about me for a few seconds. Think, instead, of how many good men have been sacrificed to the political agenda of a corrupt machinery. How many potentially great social reformers have been pushed aside for refusing to bow to the will of the Council of Elders? This cancer has pushed deep into all areas of our society, from our educational institutions to our government agencies; bright minds are frustrated for refusing to bow to the will of the caucus.

Now, let's come back to my life. I was able to change society in the government agencies I served on by refusing to follow the "sid-don-look" philosophy of the committees and instead doing what I considered right in the circumstances. Today, the reality of these government agencies has proven me right. But that is just me—an individual—within a defined environment. How do I face the larger society and tackle the same problem I faced in the government bodies? The tasks seem difficult and either divine intervention or drastic human action is required for any kind of change to happen. God, unfortunately, will not solve our problems for us—and so I have decided to take drastic action.

Senator Boniface looked at his wristwatch and surveyed his audience with calm. His listeners were slowly metamorphosing into a sea of angry and disbelieving faces and a perceptible murmur was beginning to build. A few people were on their feet, a number of whom were being physically restrained by their neighbours. Excited chatter soon replaced the murmur and for a moment, it seemed an upper-class riot would follow.

Senator Boniface raised his glass conciliatorily until there was some quiet before he continued speaking: *But what is drastic action? Take the case of the former Speaker who was shot some time ago. We all called the killer mad, but now, I see what he did and what it symbolized. I have now proposed an elaboration of the theme. Several minutes ago, I had everyone not connected with party business sent out of the building. Unfortunately, I could not give everyone present here the opportunity to put their houses in order and still achieve my intentions. You see, in about three minutes, explosive devices set within the hall and underneath the tables will go off and hopefully bury us all in the process, thereby destroying the handiwork of the political machinery in the past twelve years. There is no escape from here, the doors are sealed. Instead, let us sit back and contemplate the sacrifice we are about to make for our country's progress—probably the most selfless act many of us have ever—*

The mad scramble for the doorway by the suddenly aroused audience drowned the rest of the Senator's words. The mass of prodding, shoving, pushing, and fighting figures was a direct contrast to the pomp and wealth displayed earlier in the day. Glasses were broken and seats were shunted aside in panic. But almost as soon as the scramble began, the first in a series of explosions that would last well into the night went off. The tables exploded in glorious flame and noise.

Senator Lawrence Boniface stood quietly, like an Old Testament prophet appeasing a vengeful God; like Sango over the insurgents of Oyo, he stood, silently amused as he watched the destruction of the country's political strong room. The glass in his hand shimmered in the flame light: a macabre dance, a microcosmic copy of the explosion, reflecting in his drink. He watched quietly as the walls crashed like a traumatised box. The flames engulfed the hall caressingly, the noise of the explosions drowning out the frantic cries of the trapped occupants. And when his turn came, Senator Boniface accepted the end, standing solidly, with the satisfaction of a man who had done his duty.

The final party hosted by Senator Lawrence Boniface would be remembered for decades to come.

Gods

I stepped in a field of gods
Rows and rows of wondrous gods
Seated and standing in mass array
Supreme directors of earth's affairs
Representatives of all glory
Entouraged in moonlight glow
Issuing commands to men below

They reigned extant in discordant harmony
Some silent and weak, others dying
And still more preserved in majesty
Thousands of gods from all people
Thousands of gods in diverse battles
Wounded by the death of worshippers
Sacrificed on the altars of holy wars

Apis, Banebdjedet, and Ba-Pef
Geb, Hemen, Horus, Hu
Thoth, Weneg, Wepwawe, Wosret
Ishtar, Marduk, Nabu, Nanshe
Matronae, Modron, Morrígan, Set
Sango, Oya, Ogun, Yemoja
Zeus, Apollo, Hermes, Aphrodite
Nodens, Nudd, Nuada, Rosmerta
Aken, Ankt, Apophis, Amun
Yuanshi, Lingbao, Daode, Tianzun

Gods of space and Gods of time
Of harvest, planting, plenty and famine
Of bronze and copper, gold and stone
There were One Gods and Trinities
Gods lonely and God families
Gods with strange exotic rituals
Gods—male, female and impossibly more
Benevolent, jealous, despotic—all of man's nature

I shivered and wondered
Sought understanding of the dread vision
So many Gods seeking belief
So many Gods in need of worship
Then a wise old God came to me
Winked with a smile and whispered this:
"Doubt we all if thou must do
But always still, believe in you."

THIRTEEN:
The Apotheosis of Bishop Okikiola

"In fact, there are eggs and there are eggs.
Same thing with prophets."

WOLE SOYINKA, *THE TRIALS OF BROTHER JERO*

"This is the story of a church and of the man who
would use its influence to shape his society."

KAYODE COKER, INTRODUCTION, *BUILDING THE TEMPLE:*
THE VISION OF ETEM INTERNATIONAL.

PART 1: BUILDING THE TEMPLE

I. The Days of Small Beginnings

ETEM International, one of the largest modern Pentecostal churches in Africa, and possibly the world, had begun its missionary journey in the early seventies as a small sect with the more vengeful name of The Last Day Church of Christ's Judgment, itself a breakaway faction of the spiritualist *Aladuras* of the Celestial Church of Christ. Under the guidance of the loud and fiery Prophet Samuel, a revered *Aladura* of the Celestial Church, the faction had wiped the dust of their parent church off their white garments and proceeded to plant their bare feet in the then virgin sands of the Lagos Bar Beach. The ragtag band of 15 bible-shaking, hymn-singing members gathered

145

every morning and evening at a breezy spot along the Bar Beach to raise their voices to the horizon and prophesy doom if the nation did not turn away from its sins. These open-air services went on for about a year. Then, sometime in 1975, Prophet Samuel, in a rash move predicated by a pessimistic outlook and poor judgment, prophesied to his small congregation that the end of the world would occur in 1976.

Luckily, the world did not end in 1976. What did end, was the life of the Head of State, General Murtala Mohammed as well as the open-air services on the beach. The general was assassinated by disgruntled members of his armed forces and, in the clampdown that followed, the succeeding government went after the conspirators with a bloodlust rivalled only by the civil war of the previous decade. Unappreciative of the prayers of Prophet Samuel and his members, Bar Beach was converted into the venue for the gruesome public executions of the convicted conspirators. The stunned worshippers fled the soil that had suddenly gone from holy ground to a shooting range for firing squads.

Prophet Samuel was forced to seek tenancy for his church on the Lagos mainland, and he found help through Benjamin Okikiola, a young man of 20 whom he had converted during an encounter at the beach. Benjamin had just been admitted into the University of Lagos to study accounting, and was at a stage in life where he had become disillusioned with the domestic philosophies he grew up with. Benjamin had been impressed with the Prophet's forceful denunciation of the immoral society of the '70s. While he was not entirely convinced of the reality of the fires of hell that awaited sinners, Benjamin saw no reason why he should not be on the safe side.

Benjamin convinced his mother—a wealthy Lagos socialite and businesswoman—to lease the Prophet an unused classroom in the compound of her private primary school at a price considerably below the commercial rates. The Last Day Church of Christ's Judgment had found a new home. The Prophet and his members got to work, remodelling the classroom to suit their purpose while redefining the spiritual tenets that guided the now physically sheltered church.

Since new accommodations will always bring new expenses, Prophet Samuel was forced to begin a barefoot campaign to seek out new members for his church in the adjoining neighbourhood. But Lagos of the late '70s was unkind to a spiritually inclined agenda. The oil boom had ensured that money was plentiful. These were the days of "perms" and "afros", and nights of colourful mini-skirts and flared trousers jigging on the saturated floors of disco joints. This was the time when the Head of State could declare, "The only problem Nigeria has is how to spend the money she has."

These were the golden years of the country.

In those days, the society that Prophet Samuel sought to convert looked on the spiritual with disdain. Even the old Gods had been abandoned, and "Festac 77" had driven home the fact that traditional spirituality could be transformed into African fine art to be appreciated without dread in a gallery of art works.

Prophet Samuel's pockets were overstretched. The tithes and offerings of the faithful could not sustain the mission and by the early '80s, the Prophet – then in his late fifties – began to think of calling it quits. He communicated his despair to Benjamin, who had become his crutch in the administration of the church.

The young man listened to the Prophet's lamentations and went home in serious thought. The next day, he quit his job with a savings and loans bank in Yaba and took up spiritual apprenticeship under the Prophet. Prophet Samuel was shocked at this decision, but Benjamin convinced his mentor of the spiritual origin of his decision. He did not add, however, that having analysed his mentor's methods, he was certain that it was the Prophet's poor management style that was responsible for the failure of the church.

The Prophet took Benjamin under his wings in an intensive one-year spiritual tutelage and thereafter, on a Sunday morning in

1984, Benjamin was ordained as Prophet and Apostle of the Last Day Church of Christ's Judgement. He settled into his new role with vigour, painstakingly administering the secular affairs of the church in as detailed a manner as only an accountant could. He drew up church attendance registers, structured the tithing process, organised the now fifty-plus members of the church into small working groups, kept books of accounts and tracked the economic progress of the members to determine who deserved roles of financial responsibility. He also convinced his mother to become a member of the church, and prompted her, "by the leading of the Holy Spirit" to sell the entire school building to the church at a bargain.

II. Ten Years of Plenty

By the late '80s, Benjamin—now married—had completely taken over the administration of the church and Prophet Samuel was content to only play a spiritual role. This state of affairs contented both men until sometime in 1989 when, after reading a few books by Kenneth E. Hagin, an American preacher, Apostle Benjamin decided that the church's spiritual doctrine needed to be redefined in order to move forward more profitably. He decided to become Pentecostal.

"Rubbish! Utter nonsense!" Prophet Samuel screamed. "The river that forgets its source shall dry up, how can you forget our anteced-ents and claim for yourself a foreign ideology? We are *Aladura* in origin, we wear white garments and we go barefoot while in those garments. You cannot change that!"

"But, sir, I have a revelation from God. Don't forget that we are to worship in spirit and in truth. We walk by faith not by sight. The white garment and the bare foot are useless if we cannot perform the physical miracles Christ performed. Faith is what matters and we have to adopt Pentecostal principles to exercise this faith more usefully. This is the direction the Church is heading, a revival of faith is in progress and we have to be a part of it."

"I will hear no more of this! The man who runs faster than his God will meet an untimely end. You are speaking heresy and if you keep at it, I will excommunicate you." And with that, the venerable old man dismissed his protégé from his presence.

About a month later, the testimonies of witnesses who had watched Benjamin perform a miracle caused a minor stir in the church's vicinity. The church went wild-eyed as an apparently bedridden man jumped up from a stretcher, looking fit and healthy, after being brought in to the church for prayer. Prophet Samuel was not amused; he reprimanded Benjamin severely for what he labelled cheap theatrics and banned him from further public display of "miracles".

Benjamin took a deep breath, and then told the man who ordained him to go to hell:

"I would not allow you to drag this church down with your dogmatic, stubborn-headed and old-fashioned ideology. Take a look at the new churches around us, they understand the modern Lagosian, and they capitalise on that understanding. Why do you think you cannot get a strong foothold in a city as lively as Lagos? Because of your archaic beliefs. Why would a civil servant walk barefoot to church, much less an engineer or a lawyer? These people are proud Lagosians, eager to showcase their education! I know them; I've worked with them. To the Jews you have to be a Jew, to the Lagosians, you have to be a Lagosian.

"Our beliefs are useless if they do not impact on the people we claim we are reaching out to. We need to bring these people to God and we need them to eat. Give us this day our daily bread only makes sense when there are people to bake the bread. I am showing you a vision and you are too blind to see it. If you are not ready to follow this new pattern sir, I will have you declared insane and locked up for good. I will not allow you to destroy this church." Benjamin concluded with venom.

Prophet Samuel was taken aback.

The shock of his own former apprentice turning against him gave him a near fatal stroke and he was advised by the doctors to resign from active ministry. Retrogressing to the centuries of African beliefs buried deep beneath the layers of Christianity, he cursed Benjamin with the evils of the most dreaded Gods of the Yoruba pantheon before succumbing to a final fatal stroke.

Benjamin, unperturbed, interpreted the death of the old Prophet as divine approval of his own agenda, and he set about refashioning the church. He hired lawyers to register the church under the new name of End Time Evangelical Mission and began a series of door-to-door evangelising missions. The early '90s saw a huge surge in membership as the energetic pastor, having discarded the title of Prophet, remodelled the church in Pentecostal fashion.

He had a target of registering 500 members and he did not relent in his daily visitations until he registered the 511th member of the church. Recognising the motivating role of official titles in Nigerian society, he appointed council members, deacons and deaconesses, choir leaders, and heads of departments. He also had four assistant pastors whom he personally schooled in biblical theology – as he understood it. Meanwhile, he enrolled for a correspondence course at the Christ for the Nations Institute in Texas and soon obtained a Diploma in Divinity. Two years later, he also obtained a Doctorate in Divinity from the Oral Roberts University in the United States.

III. The Years of the Cankerworm

Trouble arrived in 1993. Economic depression and political crisis had led to a decline in church attendance. Inflation had wrecked the once carefree city of Lagos and a lingering fuel scarcity had minimised movement around the city. Money was scarce, and Benjamin – now Dr. Okikola– could see the twenty-odd years of work that he had put into his church about to crumble.

Desperate to prevent the church's imminent collapse, Dr. Okikiola launched a revival campaign. Fliers and posters were circulated around Lagos, and he introduced new terminologies over the airwaves: *Crusade! Revival!* His theory was simple: If the people could not come to the church, the church would go to the people. He organised late night crusades and revivals in soccer fields and market squares. His new message for the people who were groaning under a repressive military regime was now one of retribution and hope. The present economic paralysis and political stalemate was the evidence of God's anger at the moral decay of the '70s and '80s. He would thunder through the loudspeakers:

God's judgment is here! Put aside your earrings! Cover your heads! Shave your Afros! Wipe off your shameless lipsticks! Throw out your high heels! Repent! These are the years of the locust and the cankerworm, the years of the caterpillar and the palmerworm, God's great army that had been sent among you. God is just and God is righteous. The iniquity of the people is an affront to God, and he visits the iniquity of the fathers onto the children, but God is also merciful. He welcomes those who come to him and he forgives those who seek his forgiveness.

The first of these "crusades" had resulted in the visibly shaken attendees, moved by the passion of the preacher, wailing and crying for God's mercy, as they rolled on the floor, their hearts in despair over the loss of the good days of Lagos. The spiritual message fed off from the communal misery. When the collection box was passed around, the congregation hastily parted with their money as though they were getting rid of its sinful habitation of their purses and pockets.

It was a good start to the crusade agenda. At the end of every such crusade, Dr. Okikiola would nod appreciatively as the Head Usher gave him the total of the offerings collected. The accounts had to be balanced.

With each crusade and revival event, Dr. Okikiola opened new branches of his church, to be overseen by pastors who reported directly to him. Taking a cue from his own relationship with the late Prophet Samuel, he did not leave the administration of the branches in the hands of the branch pastors. Membership attendance, tithes, offerings and other revenue received were to be accounted for, and reports made to the headquarters on a weekly basis. Salaries and emoluments of the branch pastors and workers were also handled by the headquarters. Dr. Okikiola made sure he left nothing to chance; *faith was one thing, stupidity was another.* The old classroom building in Yaba had been pulled down and a contribution drive for a new church building was underway.

The military years of the '90s were a period of boom for spiritual activity—especially for the Christian Church. It had become socially rewarding to be considered a "born-again Christian." The stigma attached to the religion from its introduction to the West African coast and up to the late '80s had finally disappeared. Churches were springing up *en-masse* and the period saw a rapid conversion to the faith as the relevance of the old orthodox churches waned and the new churches gradually assumed a more socially acceptable role. Unable to afford the excessive bills of good hospitals, society— including the medical doctors—practically resorted to faith healing. Miracles proliferated—the dead were raised, the cripples walked, the blind received sight and the dumb could speak. Testimony sessions became a part of church culture, as preachers strove to draw the needy multitudes to their churches. Pastors became the guiding philosophers on all aspects of social life—from the education of their members to issues of marriage and family life. "Pastor", once a derogatory term for a pious but naïve person with a holier-than-thou attitude had become a title that attracted respect and honour and one which a number of established professionals were eager to append before their names.

Dr. Okikiola's church expanded rapidly during the revival era. The church purchased buses for missionary and evangelism voyages into other parts of the country. Members of the church who left Lagos were mandated to start new branches of the End Time Evangelical Mission in their new locations and not seek other churches to attend. Raising a family was encouraged: men were urged to bring in wives from outside the church, while the women were encouraged to take husbands from within. Every generation was groomed to hand over the principles and responsibilities of the church to the next. Dr. Okikiola understood that too many churches had been destroyed because the youth were neglected, and so he ensured that he attended every major youth event, and several minor ones, thus securing the love and admiration of his young church members.

He did not realise it consciously, but Dr. Okikiola had begun to dream of having the greatest church in the country.

IV. The Days of the Latter Rain

Democratic government was restored in 1999, and with the exit of the military from government, Dr. Okikiola was to become the spiritual, moral and secular adviser to a state governor, few commissioners, a number of permanent secretaries, several top civil servants and numerous other professionals. The church became the meeting point for the *nouveau riche* of Lagos as well as the upper, and aspiring, middle class. Dr. Okikiola had also cultivated his own political skills and was now an influential executive of the Pentecostal Fellowship of Nigeria, with his eye on the presidency of this powerful association. He wrote religious columns in newspapers and commissioned a plethora of television and radio shows to ensure that thousands of households around the country were familiar with his voice and features. His new message was one of prosperity—and with the evidence of the new cars in the parking lots of his church and house—it was not a hard sell.

By the year 2006, Lagos was once more a booming commercial centre, but in a more cautious way. The nightclubs and the cinemas now competed for clientele, while the churches were overflowing. The pastors interpreted the new prosperity as a gift from God with the caveat that anyone who sought to partake of it had to be willing to give to "the house of the Lord" and work for God. The Church Spiritual had become the Church Material and the role of government had been taken up by religion. The prayers that streamed towards the heavens on Sundays were requests for blessings and deliverance from poverty. A church bubble was inevitable and thousands of churches sprang over the landscape of Lagos, their doors continuously open to new members.

In the midst of these, Dr. Okikiola, a methodical and careful strategist planned his blossoming empire with the skill of a warlord. Wayward pastors were dismissed with ruthless discipline, their social reputations forcefully tarnished in the process. The church was grouped into regional zones under pastors who reported to him on the activity of each zone. Under each zone was a state pastor who was responsible for administering all the branches in each state. Dr. Okikiola was not a lazy overseer. He scrutinised the reports from every branch in unforgiving detail. If a branch did not have enough members or revenue to justify the expense of a pastor, he dismissed the pastor and had it converted to a home fellowship.

He had a separate administrative network for schools and campuses. Recognising the need to encourage the enthusiasm of youth, he allowed a more relaxed moral attitude for the younger members of his congregation. Sagging jeans, neck chains, waist beads, body hugs, spaghetti tops and other fashionable forms of dressing in a variety of designer labels became a regular feature of the dress culture of the church. This relaxed approach encouraged more youths to join—it had become fashionable to be a Christian.

He rebranded the church and it was renamed ETEM International, the original apocalyptic implications banished into the church's historical records. No one wanted to be reminded of the end time, and "prosperity forever" had become the new philosophy. The eagerness to escape the memories of the brutal military era erased the sermons of hell and the lake of fire completely. Gone were the dreadful warnings of God's wrath, judgment and eternal damnation. The church was here to stay and the church was here to be profitable. The prosperous members of ETEM were generous with their donations, and so the Bishop was able to secure choice land on the Lagos-Ibadan Expressway to build a vast auditorium that could accommodate the faithful worshippers. The last Sundays of every month were the days he personally took to the pulpit to bless his congregation, and the resulting traffic on the expressway on those Sundays had become customary, an accepted fact of the transportation system.

Eventually, Bishop Dr. Okikiola made a bid for the presidency of the PFN, and with the approval of a majority of the other powerful pastors, he obtained it. He was now, officially, the most influential religious leader in the country, and his church, the most prestigious. The position brought him international political and religious acclaim. He dined with the Catholic Pope, and corresponded with the Archbishops of the Anglican Communion. The Last Day Church of Christ's Judgment had come a long way, and Dr. Okikiola was determined, even more than anyone could have guessed, to maintain the vision that he had conceived for his church.

PART 2: A TIME FOR WAR

I. The King That Knew Not Israel

Bishop Okikiola lay in bed, sitting in an almost upright position, his back propped against the stack of pillows behind him. He clasped and unclasped fingers as he stared ahead at the mirror on the wall opposite him, seeing nothing in the mild darkness. The huge Ikoyi mansion he inhabited was silent except for the roar of the power generator, itself a background noise of the night and therefore unnoticed. His entire family was away on vacation, soaking up the Dubai sunshine. Members of his domestic staff were in their quarters and the usual retinue of relatives and acolytes that made use of his house as a temporary base were happily diminished this night. This rare solitude gave him the auditory space to arrange his thoughts, for he had a lot to think about. The issue that was depriving him of sleep was one that threatened thirty-five years of careful plans and fulfilled dreams. The Bishop was faced with one final challenge before his dream of building the greatest church in the country could be accomplished.

A wave of regulatory reforms was sweeping through Lagos as part of the agenda of the newly inaugurated state government; and while environmental, infrastructural and other social innovations were welcomed and supported by the church—his church—the latest brainwave of the government was causing the Bishop both mental and physical ulcers. It seemed impossible, but it was true—the state government wanted to regulate religious activities in the same way the federal government regulated corporate commercial activities.

This evil, Bishop Okikiola thought, as he sighed audibly, had begun with the campaign speeches of the then governorship candidate—a man with a strong sense of social justice – and so the Bishop had been wary of endorsing him. Even as an aspirant, the governor had complained repeatedly about the traffic situation on the expressways and the need to regulate the activities of the churches contributing to the problem. Soon after his election into office, the governor had created a new ministry and appointed a Commissioner for Religious Affairs, a successful lawyer and self-professed theologian. The Commissioner's first action, working with the national broadcasting commission, had been to secure a ban on the airing of miracles on television which the commission stated were performed *"in a way which are not provable and believable"*, on the premise that a lot of charlatans were using the medium to dupe innocent citizens.

Bishop Okikiola had watched the situation unfold in silence. He was himself averse to the new-fangled churches that dotted the landscape and bought television airtime for undisguised advertising. A few of the Pentecostal stakeholders had raised some outcry but the protests soon petered out. The success of this ban only emboldened the Commissioner for more regulatory actions.

Soon afterwards, the Bishop's sources in the government had brought him the eventual bad news. The Commissioner was preparing to sponsor a bill before the State House of Assembly. The Bishop had seen a draft of the proposed bill and had been horrified at its implications. It was a church regulatory bill that sought to prescribe standards on appointment of church officers, location of churches, membership size and the conduct of evangelism, while also requiring the registration of churches and taxation of church income.

Taxation. Even now, alone in bed, Bishop Okikiola's financially erudite mind recoiled at the very thought of imposing a tax on the house of God.

Soon after he heard the news, he had summoned a secret meeting of the inner caucus of the PFN to discuss the creeping threat. The meeting did not achieve much beyond a unanimous resolution by the angered church leaders that the PFN would forcefully oppose the action of the state government. But Bishop Okikiola needed more than mere resolutions. If the PFN was not successful in lobbying against the passage of the bill, ETEM International was going to be hit badly and he was not going to wait and see that happen.

He sighed again and with much effort, dragged himself to the edge of the bed and stood. He went over to the small refrigerator in the corner of the room, opened it and brought out a small bottle of brandy. He paused for a moment, and then he returned the bottle and brought out a bottle of water instead. He turned on the light switch in the room as if to make sure what he was holding was, indeed, water. He had no problem with drinking alcohol, albeit privately—the Old Testament God had expressly commanded the Jews to take strong drink—but he needed his head clear this night.

And so Bishop Okikiola stood in his room, looking at his reflection in the mirror, drinking water from the bottle and thinking about his problem. He reflected on the period, way back in the '70s, when the church was just another institution within the control of the state. But gradually, the church had assumed more social powers and now existed above and separate from the workings of the political system. This growth had been subtle and only few people were discerning enough to recognise the growing powers of the church. The Commissioner was one of such people and his ambition was to curtail that power.

But the Commissioner had come to office decades too late; Bishop Okikiola smiled to himself in the mirror. In the present decade, the church now controlled the people, a people that had lost faith in their government. It was now left to him, as the official head of the biggest churches within the country to show the government exactly what kind of powers the church wielded.

There was a time to kill and a time to heal. A time to love and a time to hate. A time for war and a time for peace.

This was the time to kill, the time to hate, the time for war. The weakness of the church was that it had become too lenient, too permissive. In contrast, the Muslims, especially in the northern part of the country, wielded much power over the state, and now it was the turn of the church to be equally militant.

The Bishop smiled at himself again and then turned towards his bed, finally getting the peace of mind he needed to sleep, he now knew what to do. But first, he would arrange a meeting with the Commissioner.

He switched off the lights.

II. Fulfilling All Righteousness

The Commissioner was referred to in the newspapers as a progressive who had little time for religious sentiments or traditional values that stood in the way of social development. He happily acknowledged this public accolade to himself, even as he stepped into Bishop Okikiola's office. He had no time for sentiments indeed, but he had long admired Bishop Okikiola's skills as an administrator; he had agreed to a meeting with the Bishop primarily out of respect for his office, but also out of curiosity about what the Bishop had to say that could persuade him to change government policy.

The man of government had come to see the man of God.

The Commissioner did not waste time on pleasantries when the two met in the Bishop's office. His tone was brisk.

"Sir, I know why you want to see me. Please do not let me waste your time; there is no going back on this policy. It is meant to be."

The Bishop considered the other man carefully, as though weighing his words against the man's ability to receive them.

"It is meant to be, you say. Tell me, Commissioner, do you believe in fate?"

The Commissioner's expression was quizzical. "Fate?"

"Yes, fate. I do not take statements like yours lightly. You say this is meant to be, so be patient, and let's examine the nature of things that are meant to be."

"Well, only if you want to have that conversation, sir. If possible though, I will rather not waste your time. My mind is made up on this matter."

"Alright then, shall I get you a glass of something to drink? This may be a long conversation—forgive me, but once I start, I have the tendency to get carried away with my own rhetoric."

The Commissioner shook his head but the Bishop was not looking at him. Instead, he reached towards a cupboard beside his desk and brought out a decanter of whisky and two small glasses. He placed these on the table and then poured out the drinks. He pushed one of the glasses across the table to the other man and then leaned back against his chair, reflectively. The Commissioner shifted in his seat, uncomfortable at the brazen display of alcohol, but the Bishop gave no indication that anything was amiss.

"As a theologian, issues of fate and predestination constantly come up in my studies—and there is a natural conflict between the idea of a God who can do all things and who knows all things on one hand and the concept of freewill and punishment on the other hand. So, for example, why would God punish a man for a sin that the man was destined to commit? Why should Judas suffer for betraying Christ?

"And here is another aspect of the issue—the occurrence of evil. Is evil fated or is it chosen? These are difficult questions for the average theologian—and you, in my opinion, are no theologian. But I wouldn't trouble you to look for answers. Instead, I will tell you my conclusion on these questions, and explain to you why I don't think your reforms are, to use your words, *meant to be*."

The Bishop leaned forward and picked the glass in front of him. He tossed its contents into his mouth and leaned back again with a smile on his face. The Commissioner glanced at his wristwatch and then at the ornate clock hanging on the wall of the room, he crossed his legs and then uncrossed them again. He had not touched his glass of whisky.

"You see, most people consider God as Omniscient," the Bishop continued. "Indeed, God knows all of the past in its totality, and He knows all of the present too. But God does not know the future—or at least, He does not permit himself to know the future. Don't get me wrong; God knows the future to the extent that it involves natural events, governed by the laws of physics—where the rain would fall, the next tsunami, the destruction of the world, even. But if God knows the future in the general sense—the sense that He knows the choices a man will make—then every person's life is predestined, and individual responsibility is abolished. Instead, God leaves the future open, variable, flexible. The future is not a single straight line; it is several diverging lines, branching in different directions, lading to even more choices. Anything can happen depending on an individual's choices. Now, each choice has its own effect and while God cannot predict your choice, He is able to foresee the effect of the choices you decided to make.

"And that's why Biblical and modern prophecies are variables not absolutes. We tell you what happens 'if' you do something, and not 'when' you do something, because we do not know if you will or will not, and neither does God.

"Therefore, Mr. Commissioner, in the end, nothing is meant to happen—instead, it is up to you, as an individual to decide what happens next. The decisions are variable and are yours to make, but the effects of those decisions are certain and beyond your control. Now, back to our original topic. I cannot say whether or not you will change your mind, but I can tell you what will happen *if* you continue with this course of yours. You will die."

The Bishop reached forward and picked up a Bible from the stack of documents on his desk, opened to a page and pushed the Bible towards the Commissioner before leaning back into his chair.

"Now, you may think I am being melodramatic. But take a look at the highlighted verse, the book of Psalms: chapter 144, verse 1. Blessed be the Lord, my rock, who trains my hands for war, and my fingers for battle."

He paused to allow the Commissioner read the text before he continued. "That scripture is profound, it has always fascinated me greatly. I have found in it the inspiration for my strength over the years. It is also inspiration for my defences against your current course of action. Of course, modern Christians are too squeamish in the face of violence, but when required, God has always been an initiator of violence upon the heathen."

The government man looked at the clergyman in continued silence.

The Bishop continued: "You are the heathen and you and I are on opposing sides of a war that you have initiated. You want to control the church, but you forget that the church has grown beyond the ability to be controlled by human government. Unfortunately, the church itself is ignorant of its power over the state. But I have a solution to that—a conflict is required to awaken the power of the church, and you, sir, have provided the means to create the necessary conflict."

The Commissioner was silent. Internally, he fumed at the Bishop's condescending tone, but he maintained an outward calm, his expression conveying an attempt at understanding the Bishop. Bishop Okikiola was heading towards a point and the Commissioner wanted to know what it was.

The Bishop leaned forward a third time, opened a drawer and pulled out a small handgun. He lay this on the table.

He looked at the Commissioner with a calm menace, waiting for the shock of the weapon to register before he continued. "This is a physical weapon. If this were a physical battle, my natural inclination would be to shoot you dead, right now. There would be no fuss at all. You are a cancer in the society and you should be removed. But this is not physical, and besides that would be too easy a way out of this for you, you will be absolved of responsibility in this issue and I don't want that."

Bishop Okikiola had gotten the gun from a grateful Deputy Commissioner of Police who believed the Bishop had cured him of a benign cancer. Even now as he looked at it gleaming on the desk, he felt an excited rush of power. There was an effect that such a weapon had on the average psyche, and he could sense the man opposite him shrinking away from the gun on the table. Physical action had more impact than mere scriptures.

The word and the sword.

"Instead," Bishop Okikiola continued, "mark my words, unless you withdraw the bill and cancel your anti-Christian policy within the next few weeks, I repeat this again, you will die." The Bishop paused and smiled. "Thus says the Lord."

The two men stared at each other with unfeigned mutual dislike. The Commissioner struggled to reconcile the public image of the Bishop with that of the man who had just threatened his life subtly, and he simply couldn't. He looked away, a cold feeling of fear building within his spine, but as soon as it came, it was quickly replaced by anger. He remembered that his police escort was within distance — and his annoyance grew into full confidence. Nothing could happen to him in the Bishop's premises. He struggled up to his feet and looked at the Bishop calmly.

"There was once a time in the history of Africa when falling in battle was more honourable than living in fear. Today, many Nigerians have forgotten what it means to fight a war to the death. I have not. Whether issued by spiritual or physical forces, I don't care about your threats, sir. That bill will be passed into law."

Bishop Okikiola kept smiling as the Commissioner left the room, his eyes now on the gun, admiring the detail of the barrel.

III. Attacking the Amalekite

Bishop Okikiola was confident of the society he presided over. Nigerian logic was a flexible one where legal and natural rules became inapplicable when "the God factor" was introduced into an argument. Within the next few weeks, the Bishop began a subliminal coaxing of his congregation. His messages were of retribution and justice, of blood and fire, and his congregation took it with the ease of people accustomed to a forthright preacher. He gave media interviews that encouraged his Christian listeners to rise in violent protest—in the name of God—against "Anti-Christian" measures by the government.

The Bishop's threat against the Commissioner was not an idle one. He had carefully thought out the psychological ramifications of a Christian uprising against the government and he believed that the best way to underscore the importance of the Church—and prevent future governments from messing around with it—would be to get rid of the Commissioner in a dramatic and spiritually significant manner. His mission was to plant the seeds that would, at worst, propel the state into suicidal conflict with the church and, at best, discourage the state from such conflict.

"The Commissioner for Religious Affairs is possessed of the devil, he is a vessel of Satan and he has now found a way to destroy the church. He has set this destruction process in motion." The Bishop said during one of such interviews.

"What we have before us is exactly what Apostle Paul meant when he said we do not wrestle against flesh and blood, but against the rulers, against the authorities, and against spiritual wickedness in high places. Unfortunately, today we wrestle also against flesh and blood, a very determined one. The Antichrist's existence is driven by the destruction of the achievements of the church. His sole purpose is defined by uprooting the church; without this, he cannot be successful. Such a man cannot be prayed for, pleaded with or persuaded to change his mind. Like the Pharaoh of Moses, he is an obstacle to the church of God and he is destined to perish.

"In Old Testament times, such a cancer in the assembly of God would have been struck by the fire of heaven. Brethren, we need the fire of heaven today. Read 2 Chronicles 15:12-13: The Israelites entered into a covenant to seek the Lord, with all their heart and soul; and everyone who would not seek the Lord, the God of Israel, is to be put to death, whether small or great, whether man or woman. Remember Achan who defied the commandments of God and how he brought about God's anger on the children of Israel! The bible says: *he who is taken with the devoted thing shall be burnt with fire, he and all that he has, because he has transgressed the covenant of Jehovah, and because he has done a disgraceful thing in Israel.* The bible says this also: And from the days of John the Baptist until now the kingdom of heaven suffereth violence, and the violent take it by force. And as for the Commissioner, I have only one prayer: *'Let his days be few; and let another take his office'.*"

◈

IV. A Time to Kill

There were two fatalities recorded from the conflict between the Church and the State. The first death was that of the Commissioner. Barely a month after his meeting with the Bishop, the Commissioner was shot and killed by a lone gunman, who then voluntarily gave himself up to the police. The killer attributed his action to divine instructions. According to the interrogation transcripts—which found their way into the tabloids—the killer indicated that he had gone to the Commissioner's estate home to preach to him and convert him from his erroneous ways, but the government man had transformed into a demon and attempted to kill him. His lawyers pleaded both insanity and self-defence. The judge was a superstitious fellow, and he committed the gunman to asylum. Public opinion was generally in favour of the killer, the belief being that if he was acting under God's instructions, then he had done the right thing. The superstitious aspect of whether the Commissioner was a *demon* or not was rarely debated.

In response to the strong public outcry on the issue, the state government abandoned the proposed bill. The new Commissioner for Religious Affairs was a devout Christian and a member of Bishop Okikiola's church. The ministry shifted its agenda away from religious regulation to religious harmony.

In a message to the church the Sunday following the murder, the Bishop mentioned the incident, citing it as an example of what happens when a man chooses to wage war against God—*even the devil would be unable to save him.*

"*And the one who falls on this stone will be broken to pieces; and when it falls on anyone, it will crush him,*" the Bishop quoted. "My mentor used to say: 'The man who runs faster than his God will meet an untimely end.' And you have all seen the truth of that proverb. Nothing, and I say it again, nothing can stand against the progress of the church."

V. An Eye for an Eye

It was several Sundays later, while Bishop Okikiola surveyed the 300,000 people congregated in the headquarters of his church with a pride that would have put a lion's strut to shame, that the second death occurred. On that day, the Bishop stood before his people with a sense of pride that his work was finally complete; the government had backed down on the blasphemous bill and the church had become militant.

The dull hum of the air conditioning units strategically positioned around the gaily-decorated auditorium could be heard in the brief silence as the congregation expectantly awaited the Bishop's next thunderous blessing. It was a fine day to be in church and the simple and the wealthy of Lagos had gathered on that Sunday morning inside the mega-headquarters of their church, along the Lagos-Ibadan Expressway, to celebrate the thirty-fifth anniversary of the sprawling ETEM empire and also launch the enthusiastic biography of the Bishop: *Building the Temple: The Vision of ETEM International*. ETEM was now a church of over 200 branches in 20 international cities, dozens of towns, and scores of villages and hamlets welded in a unifying love for and homage to the one man who put it all together.

Amongst the congregation that celebratory Sunday was an unusual worshipper, the widow of the late Commissioner. Her purpose in church was of a less spiritual inclination. She was a simple but educated woman who understood the words of Achebe when he wrote: *you died a good death if your life had inspired someone to come forward and shoot your murderer in the chest without asking to be paid*. She had read those words again after the death of her husband. A *good death*. Those words had kept haunting her. The consequences of her loyalty was one the Bishop's calculations had not considered, and so after she reached the front of the church to deposit her thanksgiving offering into the black offering box, she went up the dais and knelt in prayer at the Bishop's feet, brought out a small gun from her purse, and shot Bishop Dr. Benjamin F. Okikiola, the Presiding Bishop and General Overseer of ETEM International.

The Thesis

I am the Superman...

No mere mortality equalises me
for my spirit transcends even the bounds of earth.
Avaunt! The womb is but a narrow cave,
a mere shadow of the deep throne of the grave.
My flesh is survived by the works of my mind
The power around me is my stride through heaven.
Wherever I go, with me is Paradise.

FOURTEEN

A Waste of Breath

I balanced all, brought all to mind,
The years to come seemed waste of breath
A waste of breath the years behind
In balance with this life, this death

WILLIAM BUTLER YEATS, *AN IRISH AIRMAN FORESEES HIS DEATH*

"This movie you are about to see
is based on a true story."

ANONYMOUS

I. The Class Representative

It was Election Day and Ade faced the class from the lecture stage with a confident grin. The faces in the audience were a curious blend of disapproval, encouragement, boredom and mute indifference. As he rolled out his manifesto with what he considered — in his seventeen-year-old mind — his "can-do" attitude, he reflected on the circumstances that had led him to the ballot box.

He had always thought he was going to be elected as class representative unopposed. It was not so much a matter of logical certainty as it was of optimistic conviction. After all, had ne not been the one running around and doing odd jobs for the class lecturers since the beginning of the session? While they were still fresh-faced intakes into the university, he had been the one lugging the heavy public address system from one lecture room to the other, preparing the attendance register and doing all those other little things that greased the machinery of an academic class.

However, the bourgeoning policy makers of the class, the Council of Elders—a group of older men who condescended to study full-time instead of the usual part-time generally preferred by adults and working class students—announced that the class would have to hold an election to determine the class representative, instead of the natural selection Ade had expected. He was dismayed by the news. He was no firm believer in the concept of democracy. For a while, however, he believed he could contest and win without much effort, until Seun Onifade arrived on the scene.

Even school politics is not exempt from the *godfather principle*, which meant that the elected leader was determined by the financial and political strength of his backer, and Seun was well supported by able godfathers in the class who had the cash to finance his mini-campaign. And so with drinks and exotic dishes circulated among the female students—the majority gender—Seun rose from a relatively unknown person to a *popular jingo*, literally overnight. A private party, held from dusk to dawn, for some of the more worthy boys in the class sealed the popularity contest. The next day saw fully hydrated boys drunkenly rooting for Seun as the saviour of the class.

As a worried Ade saw his hopes of becoming the class rep decline with each passing day, he attempted to salvage his own candidacy by suggesting to the Council of Elders that an assistant class representative should also be elected. This deputy position was to be awarded to the person with the second highest number of votes in the election. The Council of Elders discussed with the godfathers, and then acceded to this request, bearing in mind that while Seun was malleable to their wishes, Ade was more likely to get the real work of governance done.

Now, as he rounded off his speech, Ade held on to the hope that Seun's godfathers would be defeated by good sense and he could still win the election. There were now ten contenders for the position. The other eight students had mostly joined the race either for the sake of entertaining the class or merely fulfilling their private fantasies of contesting an election and clearly had no serious belief in their own ability to win.

It was going to be an open ballot in the form of a regulated show of hands. The class register, with the names of all class members, lay open on a table in the centre of the stage. Ten other blank registers, one for each candidate, were beside the class register. The name of each candidate would be called, and then students who wished to vote for the candidate would climb up the stage to write down their names in the candidate's register and tick out their names in the class register.

Seun's name was called first. A ripple spread across the hall as over half of the class, mostly female students, stood up to put down their names for him. Ade sighed, and mentally accepted the fact that the best he could be was assistant class representative. The other candidates were called and votes were cast. At the end of the process, the votes were counted, although it was apparent Seun had won the election. When the results were announced with Seun securing about sixty *per* cent of the total votes cast, Ade turned to Seun, who was sitting smugly beside him.

"Congratulations, bro. You've won."

"Come on," Seun replied graciously, "You and I will make a pretty good team. You know I won't be able to run this class without your help." While he was speaking, it was announced that another candidate, Fred, had emerged second, beating Ade by a narrow margin. In a twist unforeseen even by the godfathers, a number of people from the Ibo bloc of the class had voted ethnically, sweeping in one of theirs as the assistant class representative.

Ade sat, stunned. He was without an official position in the class, and even as he chided himself for the selfish thoughts that swarmed his mind, he was also certain he deserved better treatment from his classmates. He had never been confident about the merits of a democratic system and now his fears had been confirmed.

He had always believed that people were too impressionable to be left with the responsibility of making social decisions. Democracy was a form of government that allowed the misinformed to exercise critical powers. His merit had been swept aside by the force of Seun's campaign. Ade recognised his foe as the democratic process, and as he sat alone, willing back the tears that seemed eager to spill over, he understood the difference between the reality of a candidate, and the perception of same. In a democracy, perception always won.

One of his male colleagues curiously asked him, "Now that you have lost the election, what are your plans for the class?"

Ade shrugged and replied: "The next year is around the corner."

Barely two weeks after the election, the class began to realise that the quality of service they were receiving from Seun was several rungs below Ade's voluntary service before the election. Seun forgot to summon lecturers, he was himself late for classes and rarely made an effort to organise class activities. In fact, although he was an excellent and charismatic socialiser, functionally, his score as an administrator was nil.

Late one night, several "concerned" members of the class came to see Ade in his room. They had prepared a petition outlining Seun's flaws and calling for his removal—high treason—and wanted Ade's vocal support. While the petition did not mention that Ade would replace him, the people at the meeting hinted at the possibility. Ade thanked them for requesting his backing. He was sure, however, that he was done with class politics for the session but would be glad to offer his services whenever requested. The coup plotters left his room, expressly stating their disappointment in his inability to seize the opportunity presented to him.

The plotters struck, and the petition was published on the class board. This act signalled the beginning of what would later be referred to as the War of the Petitions. For another month, a series of petitions and counter petitions from pro-Seun supporters and anti-Seun dissidents were put up on and torn down from the board. Despite Ade's indifference, the plotters championed him as their representative. Arguments and blows were exchanged over who would make a better class representative. Caucuses aligned and re-aligned. There were skirmishes and full-scale fights in the classroom and the hostel rooms as each faction sought to impose itself on the class—a war between seventeen-year old, testosterone pumped boys was a bloody event.

Once again, the Council of Elders stepped into the matter and insisted that the class set up a football team. The class wars were moved to the football fields. The logic of the Council of Elders worked: sides were changed so much on the field that at the end of the day, nobody knew who was a foe or enemy anymore and the prior rebellion was soon forgotten. Unfortunately for Ade, he was not sport inclined and the memory of his pre-election contributions soon became part of the general class stories. As the class settled into an eventful academic year, Seun consolidated his hold on his office and did his best to meet the demands of his electorate. He may not have been a good class representative, but he was a superb striker on the football field and that was good enough for the boys.

II. The Student Senator

In the second school year, old alliances were renewed and new ones were forged. The class had become politically active, especially because they had recently participated in the Student Union elections before going on holidays. Now, freshly resumed and no longer freshmen *jambites*, they were all eager to test their newfound maturity. Sure enough, a clamour was raised for the election of a new class rep. Seun's laxity in the previous year was again brought to the fore and examined with raised eyebrows. However, the Council of Elders were too busy fighting bigger political battles outside the class and so practically left the election of a new class rep to the care of Seun himself.

In a manner reminiscent of most African leaders, Seun promptly reconstituted himself as the *class rep* and commenced a second term in office by a simple declaration of the fact. This breach of traditional protocol was not considered surprising. When Seun contested the office in the first year, it was simply a result of the promptings of his godfathers; but having spent a year in office, he had discovered the pleasures of the fringe benefits that went with the job. There was the public goodwill that came almost inevitably, as well as an automatic seat in the Senate of the Law Society (with sitting and other amorphous allowances), the general authority to make decisions on behalf of the class, the opportunity to control the sale of lecturers' hand-outs, and the numerous "tips" from people who wanted any of several favours like submission of late assignments, filling names of absentees on the class attendance sheets, or pleading a cause before the lecturers.

Seun disliked his job, but he enjoyed the benefits, and so he remained the class rep but gradually began to delegate most of the tasks and assignments to Ade. Fred, his official assistant had quit his responsibilities at the beginning of the new session, not through any recognisable legal process, but out of a personal and sudden despair at the indignity of being regarded as Seun's assistant. It was a known fact that assistant class reps rarely partook in the social and economic benefits that the class representatives enjoyed. So he had quietly stopped doing any work, though when required, he still answered to the name of "assistant class rep", albeit reluctantly. Thoroughly disillusioned, Fred went on to face his studies squarely and was soon forgotten by the class.

Although Ade was still officially jobless, his status changed one day while in his room, reading a book. He found himself having to play host to another delegation from the class. The Council of Elders had reasoned exhaustively about the matter and having concluded that he was the best person for the job, were eager both to compensate him for his long suffering, and to have him stand for election and contest as the class representative in order to occupy the seat in the Senate of the Law Society.

"And what's the catch?" Ade asked.

"Catch? Nothing, Ade, nothing at all. You know you deserve this. The Law Society politics is not like the class politics. We need someone smart and hardworking to be our eyes and ears in the Senate of the Law Society. Come on, take this opportunity," the leader of the Council of Elders said.

Ade considered the proposition and accepted it. He had not really wanted anything to do with the Law Society, but still, it was for the benefit of his class. And with this decision, Ade was thrown into the world of campus politics and intrigues on a faculty-wide scale, while still only in his second year.

The Law Society government had three arms: the Executive, the Arbitration Council, and the Senate. Deciding who held real power between the Senate and the Executive depended largely on whether the incumbent Executive was a strong one or a divided and weak one. If the Executive was united and strong, it invariably carried the electorate along and had the full support of faculty members, in which case everyone generally disregarded the Senate's resolutions and directives, including the Senate itself. However, an Executive consisting of members from different factions was a ready prey for the Senate. Such a scenario would allow the Senate wield real power and could easily impeach any erring member of the Executive, including the President.

Before Ade's Senate could be constituted, a weak Executive, whose members constantly bickered at and undermined one another, was in place. The Senate held real power for that term and Ade was a junior backbencher of that impressive Senate.

It turned out that Ade (Senator Adesola Oyedele, the Honourable Senator from the Year Two constituency) was an acquaintance of the President of the Law Society—a weak and vacillating Year Five student who swayed with whatever opinion his domineering friends imposed. Prior to both their elections, Ade had the opportunity to work with the President on some assignments so he knew him quite well, but as soon as Ade got into the Senate, he took his job seriously—and that job included not fraternising with the Executive. He avidly followed the speeches made by the senators from the senior classes, taking notes, keeping in mind their speaking patterns and the excellent phrases they used, but he said very little himself.

Ade's eagerness to be useful caught the eye of the Senate President, a female Year Four student whose domineering personality contrasted sharply with her small and fragile-looking physical frame. She was the most powerful person in the faculty students' politics, and she promptly put Ade's zeal to good use. He would spend hours in her office, sitting on a black box that served as a chair, helping to draft sensitive and confidential correspondence while listening to her chatter about the personalities of the major dissenters in the house. Ade knew that she was attempting to brainwash him, but he listened all the same, with an open mind.

To be an outstanding legislator, a representative has to either be able to sponsor bills effectively or oppose them passionately. With the help of his new acquaintanceship with the Senate President, Ade got his first public achievement when he drafted and presented a bill for a faculty student law for the award of grants to deserving handicapped faculty students. The bill did not get passed into law, but it improved Ade's reputation considerably, and consequently brought him to the notice of other members of the legislative body.

During one of their work sessions in the Senate President's office, the young woman looked up from her desk and called Ade's attention. He was seated in front of a computer before her.

"Ade," she began, "I want you to start taking minutes of the Senate sittings, going forward. After the sittings, please forward them to me for review."

Ade was surprised. Minute taking was the constitutional and practical duty of the Clerk of the Senate, and the position was not vacant. A Year Three student held that title with proper aplomb. As far as Ade knew, nothing was wrong with the Clerk. He objected immediately but the Senate President dismissed it with a wave. "Just do as I've told you."

And so, Ade began to take minutes of Senate sittings secretly, without the knowledge of the Clerk. He knew something was afoot, but he was learning how to play politics. He took the minutes, and faithfully forwarded them to the Senate President. Delighted with his reliability, she was soon inviting him to attend secret, closed-door meetings with members of the Senate's inner circle - the true policy makers.

In these meetings, words were spoken of impeachments and removals, senators were marked down for suspension and recall, and students were nominated for one position or the other. Though he felt outraged at some of the decisions taken, Ade always kept mute; reminding himself that he was to be seen and not heard. Besides, it was all child's play—students playing at being adults, nothing to be taken too seriously.

It was during one of these meetings that the Clerk was finally marked for removal. At a first mention of the issue, the Senate President told her caucus of the scribe's recent insubordination, stating that he was apparently getting too big for his boots. The caucus considered this submission and an observation stage was declared. The decision that the Clerk should be removed was eventually taken at another midnight meeting.

In broad daylight however, there was no show of animosity between the Senate President and her Clerk, and it was with surprise that the Clerk, ignorant of the background devices, heard the motion calling for his removal read out. Another senator seconded this motion—and there was no counter motion. The Clerk made a move to counter the motion himself but he had no seconder. The resolution was passed. The Senate President launched into a silken speech about him having been a good worker, but then, she shrugged, the voice of the people was the voice of God; and in no time, a new Clerk was elected.

The new Clerk was essentially a figurehead. The Senate President promoted Ade as her personal aide and relied on him for all the clerical functions of the legislative body. By law, however, the Clerk had to come from a third year class, and so Ade could only act *de facto* and not officially.

The next person on the blacklist of the Senate's inner caucus was the feeble President of the Law Society. The Executive had shown a divided front; but the Senate, and its President, were becoming stronger with each passing month. The members of the Senate were intent on knocking this fact into the consciousness of, not just the Law Society President, but the friends and advisers that controlled and influenced him. The Senate President wanted to send a clear message, "I can remove your man—anytime".

To put these intentions into effect, the Senate opened an audit of the society's finances, calling for a statement of the Law Society financial accounts from the Financial Secretary.

Disbelieving the seriousness of the summons, the Financial Secretary, who had never kept an account of anything, ignored the directive. After a third directive was issued by the Senate and ignored by the Financial Secretary, the Senate passed a resolution freezing the accounts of the Law Society and also summoned the Financial Secretary to appear in person on the floor of the Senate and give a detailed account of the society's finances.

With impeachment threats hanging over him, the luckless Financial Secretary hurried to his office to prepare rough accounts and then went back to the floor of the Senate with the impromptu statements. The Senate had a merry time tearing apart his shoddy draft and the night's session ended with the Financial Secretary nearly in tears.

Later that night, Ade was surprised when his former acquaintance, the President of the Law Society, visited. He reminded Ade of their past relationship and urged him to "do the right thing" by openly supporting the Executive in the Senate. It was a laughable proposition, but Ade did not laugh. He thought it pathetic that the President of a respected student body had been driven so low. He advised the President to get a good statement of account ready and have it explained properly. The President looked at him incredulously, shook his head and left Ade's room.

Meanwhile, another delegation had been sent to the Senate President to plead the cause of the Executive. With feigned disinterest, the Senate President agreed to arrange a meeting between the inner caucus of the Senate and the representatives of the Executive in order to smoothen out the creases in their hitherto smooth relationship.

The mediation meeting took place the following day and Ade was part of it. The plea of the delegates from the Executive was premised around the fact that they had a big event—The Student Cultural Night—scheduled, and expenses had to be paid before the details could be finalised, but the freezing of the Law Society account had made this impossible. The arrangements would collapse unless the account was unfrozen in time. The Senate inner caucus again requested for the elusive statement of accounts, but the Executives promised to present one after the event. And so both parties reached an agreement that the accounts be unfrozen temporarily with the understanding that the Senate would be presented with a financial statement immediately after the event. This was to be finalised at an emergency Senate sitting to be held that night.

That emergency sitting was one of the worst in the annals of the Law Society. In the short period after the Senate had frozen the account of the society and summoned the Financial Secretary, there had been differing opinions among students about the issue. The rumour being spread by the supporters of the Executive was that the Senate intended to scrap the Student Cultural Night.

There was a reason why the cultural event was the focal point in the political activities of that night. The Student Cultural Night was the biggest event of the Law Society, second only to the Annual Law Dinner. In a faculty that was ostensibly geared towards intellectual pursuits and academic discipline, all members of the faculty eagerly welcomed a yearly prospect for song, dance and drama. The Student Cultural Night provided an avenue to get away from the academic tensions; it was a key part of the calendar. A fast way to become unpopular within the faculty was to stand in the way of that event.

During the emergency sitting, motions and counter motions were moved and opposed, both earnestly and in jest by members of the Senate not privy to the arrangements of the evening. These deviations caused more outcries both from the floor and the gallery. A person's hand was raised against another's face in anger, and the sitting was disrupted by supporters of the Executive.

The Senate President kept her counsel at this treachery by the Executive. She stood up after some calm had been restored to the room and advocated that the account be unfrozen for the cultural event to hold. The relevant motions were raised and adopted and jubilant faculty students carried out the members of the Executive victoriously from the sitting, shoulder high.

Ade's reputation suffered along with the generality of the Senate. At the gate of the venue for the Student Cultural Night he was even mocked by the ticket collectors. "Bloody Senator," someone said to him at the entrance. He turned away angrily, refusing to attend the event. He was yet to learn how to either assimilate or ignore insults.

After the event, the Senate with one voice demanded not only the statement of the society account, but a breakdown of the expenses incurred and revenue derived from the Student Cultural Night event. The Executive stalled, and without much ado, the Senate suspended the President of the Law Society, the Financial Secretary, the Secretary General, the Assistant Secretary General, the Social Secretary and the Treasurer. The Vice President was handed the reins of the disintegrated government pending the outcome of the investigation by the Audit Panel set up by the Senate to look into the matter.

Ade was elected secretary to the Audit Panel. As the scribe of the panel, his job was to collate the required documents from the Financial Secretary and screen them for the panel. He also signed and sent the letters requiring affected students to appear before the panel, and put up notices about the progress of the panel's investigation. While not making any major decisions in the panel, he was effectively its operational arm and so his name soon became synonymous with the Audit Panel. His prominence in the proceedings having been duly noted, friends and foes alike began to approach him to cajole, persuade, threaten, plead, or bribe him and curry favours—to no avail. However, he was sympathetic to the Financial

Secretary, who was apparently an innocent, if misguided, person in the sea of corruption that swarmed around the Executive. Ade strove to prove the Financial Secretary's innocence before both the panel and the Senate, making some of the other senators view Ade with veiled suspicion.

Meanwhile the suspended members of the Executive did not sit and mope, they rallied their supporters and went from class to class demanding the recall of the various senators, and in two weeks, they had gotten enough signatures from each of the classes to recall all the senators.

There was a little constitutional problem though. The Law Society Constitution specified that a senator could only be recalled through a petition signed by fifty members of his own class. The question was whether these same fifty people could simultaneously recall all the five senators from their class or if each senator had to be recalled independently, one at a time, with a new petition and list of names collected for each recall.

The constitutional matter was quickly referred to the student Arbitration Council who deliberated for two days before making a decision in favour of the Executive, in a controversial judgment that would generate debates for years even after the students had graduated. The Arbitration Council declared that all the senators of the Law Society should be recalled from office.

However in anticipation of this decision by the Arbitration Council, the last legal act of the Senate had been to quickly move and adopt a motion impeaching all members of the Executive once and for all. For anyone keeping scores, it stood at one-one.

The student body of the faculty was in disarray, how could there be no Executive and no Senate? That was impossible. Several self-proclaimed logicians tried to reason it out: the Senate impeaches the Executive, and the Arbitration Council decides the Senate was now recalled. This was a profound gap even the Constitution had not foreseen. There was a stalemate and so the matter was referred to the faculty staff members.

Neither the Dean of the faculty nor the Staff Adviser to the Law Society was amused by the convoluted state of affairs. The Staff Adviser called a conference of the major stakeholders during which he reminded the contending factions that they were first and foremost students, not politicians, and their activities should be to further academic aspirations and little else. Everyone was cut down to size, the Executive was restored to office and the members of the Senate were returned to their positions. The *status quo* was re-established.

A subdued Senate withdrew its support from its overreaching President, and till she graduated from the faculty, she never regained the power she once wielded. Ade was not exempted from the fall from power; he was once more consigned to the backbenches of the Senate while the Executive continued to stumble around without interference.

The end of the session came along in due course, ushering in the beginning of a new electoral process for the next government of the Law Society. Having had an inner view of the workings of the legislature, Ade decided to change sides and contest the position of Financial Secretary in the next elections.

He had worked closely with the current Financial Secretary during the audit fiasco, and he believed there were a few things wrong which he could set right, and he could also avoid the traps that the current Financial Secretary had fallen into. Even though Ade had since abandoned the internal wrangling of his own class, he still believed he had their general support. After all, he had faithfully carried out their wishes as a senator, he had brought attention to his class while serving as secretary to the Audit Panel, and one way or the other, he had made his class relevant in faculty politics.

For the second time in two years, he was convinced he was going to win an elective position on merit.

The Financial Secretary of the Law Society was required by the Constitution to be elected from the third year class. However, unlike the legislative positions, the Financial Secretary position required not just the votes of the candidates' classmates but also those of the entire faculty. Although in practice, it was the class members and not the student body that decided who won the Executive posts. This made sense, as every class was too busy supporting the candidates required from their own class to bother too much about the candidates from other classes. The result was that the rest of the faculty generally voted in the Executive candidates with the strongest votes from their own class.

Ade resigned from the Senate in order to contest the election into the new Executive, a move that brought sharp cries of betrayal from other senators. He was denounced on the floor of the legislative house and likened to a rat deserting a sinking ship with some members describing him as a turncoat and a traitor.

The members of the outgoing Executive, and their supporters, also got wind of Ade's intentions and were equally eager to malign him, jeering and taunting at every faculty corridor. There were occasional outbursts swearing that he would never win any position in the student association. They had not forgotten his role as secretary of the Audit Committee.

Ade's certainty that he would find refuge with his classmates was shaken when he realised that the Council of Elders and his more politically inclined classmates openly dissociated themselves from his campaign. He had not offended any of them, but they would not dare align themselves publicly with a political pariah. Ade had fallen out of favour with the powers of the faculty and he was to bear his burdens alone.

During the period before the election, on his bed most nights, he would ponder his actions and how he could have avoided his current political situation. For a brief period he had been certain he was headed to a leadership role and now he was being firmly rejected by everyone. When he went to classes and during other activities in the faculty, he walked with trepidation. He was still a second year student and he had managed to alienate almost every political group in the faculty.

The members of the Executive, eager to suite action to their words and splinter Ade's votes, raised three other candidates from his class to contest the post of Financial Secretary. Ade remembered his first year election contest all over again. He smiled ruefully whenever he thought of the candidacy against Seun just a year before. He was going to play the campaign game the right way this time around.

Another Election Day came around, more sophisticated than the one in his first year and much more intriguing. The results were however unambiguous, Ade won by a clear majority. He might as well have contested unopposed.

Majority of Ade's classmates, ignoring the political brokers, had not disappointed him this time around. He had done a personal and careful campaign and they had come out to vote for him. They came in trickles, but they came nevertheless, and as they came, they brought along people from the other classes whom they had persuaded to vote for him.

At the Law Dinner that ended the session, Ade was inaugurated along with members of the new Executive amidst ovation from few friends and many foes.

III. The Financial Secretary

Ade's tenure as Financial Secretary of the Law Society started on a bad note. The President of the newly constituted Law Society Executive was a supporter of the former President and, naturally, he viewed Ade with distrust and suspicion. Also reacting naturally, Ade lost his temper with him not on a few occasions. However, because of the enormity of the task of running a student body, personal animosities soon took a back seat and tasks were brought forward and allocated. There were students' dues to be collected, bank account signatories to be changed, receipts to be issued, funds to be raised, and most importantly, careful and detailed accounts to be kept. Cash had to be deposited and withdrawn, the new Senate was also being constituted and though a budget was yet to be approved, money had to be spent.

The decision about how to pay for expenses pending the approval of the budget by the yet to be constituted Senate was the first of the agonising problems that would eventually turn Ade and the new President into good friends. They decided that the unapproved money just had to be spent (with receipts to show for them, of course) and the Senate could ratify the expenses later. They were both certain that it was a reasonable decision and a reasonable Senate would surely approve of it. Privately, though, Ade shuddered when he thought of what a vengeful Senate could inflict as consequence of this bending of the rules.

The Executive government soon showed itself as a united front. They had learnt from the mistakes of the previous government. They kept their wrangling internal, and the members of the new Executive did their jobs and responded to student requests promptly. The Executive was once again gaining the respect that had been lost by the past administration.

Trouble started when the Senate was finally constituted. The budget was passed without a hitch but the Senate wanted to understand (or so it claimed) why money had been spent without prior approval. The new Senate President was a tall, calm young gentleman with an amiable look that suggested he quite understood the words being spoken to him and there was nothing to worry about. Ade liked him immediately.

On the floor of the house, Ade explained that the machinery of government would grind to a halt if the Executive had waited for the Senate to be constituted before performing all of its duties. He asked that the Senate would ratify the money spent so far, and then approve permission to spend more in the future.

The speech was reasonable but there were troublemakers from the past administration who remembered Ade and the role he had played. They flayed him with ridiculous questions until, exasperated, he burst out in anger.

"Let me remind the members of this house that I was once a senator of this faculty and I understand the workings of this Senate as much as anyone here. I therefore refuse to be intimidated by any tactics that some members of this Senate are displaying!"

The Senate President was not tickled by this outburst. He cautioned Ade and dismissed him from the Senate floor.

The outburst, however, further strengthened the bond between Ade and the Executive President. By taking a second look at things, Ade had come to realise that he had misjudged the fellow; he had turned out to be an honest and straightforward person, interested in exchanging ideas on how to improve the student lot both in the faculty and the generality of the university. At a point in their friendship, the President began to invite Ade to attend the Student Union House of Representative sittings with him.

A strong Student Union body is possibly the most powerful association in a university—and sometimes outside it. The Student Union was often much more effective at getting demands met than the staff bodies, and much better at dictating and influencing student behaviour than any other association in the university community.

By virtue of the position, Presidents of the faculty student bodies are also automatic members, *ex-officio*, of the Student Union House of Representatives—a body that was the university's equivalent of the Law Society's Senate. The President of the Law Society was not too excited about the late night sittings of the Student Union house and gradually he began to delegate the duty of attending these sittings to Ade. Ade was never shy of new responsibilities and he accepted this with enthusiasm, drawing on his observations in the sittings as combat training for the series of unending skirmishes with the Senate of his own faculty.

Back in the faculty, Ade was also proving himself to be a competent Financial Secretary. His penchant for taking responsibility soon brought other duties his way. He soon began to take over the duties of the Secretary General, a fourth year student who was only too glad to be relieved of his secretarial burdens. To this already laborious workload, Ade also added the duties of the Vice President, and soon enough, he was considered the *de facto* Secretary General and Vice President alongside his own original responsibilities. His ever-sceptical classmates wondered how he managed to maintain a fair second-class upper in his grade point average.

However, while his classmates wondered, members of the junior classes worshipped him. Ade was gaining a dedicated following of admirers among the fresh students. He was also getting well known for his characteristic openness and fair play attitude in the various matters that came his way. The Dean of the faculty, as well as the lecturers, also took note of his attitude towards responsibility and started assigning tasks to him personally, instead of the Law Society President.

Ade had discovered that the secret to rapid progress within any organisation was in the unselfish assumption of responsibilities, especially in a setting where everyone else avoided responsibility.

He performed tasks that made others speculate about his motives, as there seemed to be no obvious return from his activities. In response, Ade would constantly tell his classmates that he was developing his character—if nothing else—and that this was the most important thing in life. They would thumb their noses at the didactic explanation and he would in turn ignore the detractors, calmly assuming even more responsibilities.

His tenure in office soon ended amidst accolades, and during the handing over ceremony at the Law Society Dinner, he was lauded by the Dean and other members of staff, while the students grudgingly conferred several meritorious awards on him.

IV. The Speaker

In his fourth year, Ade turned aside from Law Society activities and decided to venture into mainstream school politics. His academics were in good standing, and his social life was shaping out fine within and outside the faculty. He had learnt to mingle with all types of people: from the serious, bible brandishing members of the Deeper Life fellowship to the hardy, marijuana smoking, *suspected* cultists.

Ade's philosophy was to understand the rationale behind human behaviour - why people acted the way they did. Once he could understand the *why*, he was less bothered about the *what*. He pronounced himself a rationalist, but he did not agree with the idea that everyone had to subscribe to the same beliefs or practice.

He was at home with the upper class, the *la Casera* girls, and he could also charm his way through a bevy of the *aristo* girls. He still had no interest in sporting activities, but he had learnt to organise teams and draw up sporting timetables for inter-class competitions. He attended the parties organised by his more sociable colleagues on Friday nights, and there he would sip a little beer and then leave when the party was in full swing. The next morning, he would be in one of the faculty classrooms soberly giving tutorials to a few students from the junior classes.

He was single, as far as students relationships went, yet he was responsible for several romantic matches in the faculty—the partners of which were eternally grateful to him—and he was a ready shoulder for heartbroken colleagues who came to pour out their tales of love's labour lost.

Most of the enemies he had made during his junior years had now graduated, and those who had not had either learnt to tolerate his philosophies or had even aligned themselves with him. He had the majority of students on his side.

Expectedly, when he decided to contest the position into the Student Union House of Representatives, the electoral process was a mere formality. He and six other students, including the new Law Society President, a friend of his from the fifth year, became the representatives of the students of the Faculty of Law to the university's Student Union House of Representatives.

If the Law Society Senate had been powerful, the Student Union House of Representatives was even more awe inspiring, or could be. It comprised of, depending on the study duration of the relevant discipline, between five and seven members from every department in the school and the numbers alone made it an intimidating organisation.

Like every democratic republican government, there was the constant power tussle between the Executive and the legislative arms of the Student Union government; either one was stronger than the other or, at best, they had equal measure of influence. This political situation was no longer surprising to Ade; he had come to expect the power play.

The leader of the House of Representatives, the Speaker, was required by the Student Union Constitution to be elected from among the representatives; he had the Deputy Speaker, the Clerk, and the Whip to officiate with him. These posts were duly contested for and elected before the House settled for business.

The first duty of the representative house was to create committees for the various areas of student activity it had to oversee. Ade was nominated into the Student Finance and Allocations Committee, and as merit dictated, he was appointed Chairman of that committee.

Committee work was not as exalting as it seemed, it involved a lot of paper shuffling and numberless night meetings, night—because meetings between members of several departments could only be held at night after lectures. Every committee operated under guidelines called "terms of reference". The terms of reference of Ade's committee included the review of the respective budgets of the Student Union Executive and the Student Union House of Representatives, the determination of House allowances, the remuneration for members of the Student Union Executive, as well as student grants. It involved everything that had to do with the spending of union money in all spheres of student activity.

The bribes came first—members of the Executive who wanted favourable recommendations and increased allocations approached Ade with suggestions, they promised kickbacks and percentages from funds to be raised if the budget could be inflated in indicated areas. They assured Ade that this was the way it had always been done.

On one hand, Ade wanted to blow the whistle and send everyone packing, but on the other hand, he had learnt over the years that political problems required political solutions. So, instead of giving expression to the furious emotions building in his veins, Ade smiled and remonstrated by telling them that he never made committee decisions single-handedly, everything had to be tabled before the other committee members, nine of them, and if they could all approve of the suggestions, there would be no problem.

The usual response to this answer often varied from puzzled smiles to angry outbursts, but it soon dawned on the potential bribers that entangling Ade in the underhand practices of the House was going to be a tough call. With this realisation, the threats began.

On the floor of the House, during a sitting, Ade stood up and asked for an opportunity to give a speech. The Speaker granted this.

"Recently, I've been receiving threats from certain persons regarding my refusal to partake in some scandalous schemes. This is my general response to all of these persons and to their agents. I am not afraid of your threats. I am used to being threatened. However as a reasonable human, intent on the preservation of my life and physical welfare, I have combined a list of the names of everyone who has offered me incentives in order to abdicate my responsibilities and I have forwarded this to the local DPO who is an acquaintance of mine.

"If anything out of the ordinary happens to me, then several of you can expect full investigations and several sleepless nights. You may think a little visit by the police is worth the gains, but remember, after you've dealt with me, you will still have all of my other committee members to contend with."

His claim to have filed a complaint with the Divisional Police Officer was a lie, but Ade believed firmly that where violence was initiated or threatened against him, a lie was a tool he could morally use to defend himself.

It soon dawned on the top members of the House of Representatives that they had made a mistake by nominating Ade into the Finance Committee. He had exhibited such a pleasant and listening attitude that they had thought him an easily persuaded fellow, and now they were thoroughly shocked to discover that beneath the soft layer was a personality of steel. However, there was nothing that could be done about this. Ade was doing a good job and as far as the majority of the House of Representatives were concerned, he was something of a folk hero and an extremely likeable person.

Affairs ran along smoothly until Ade discovered fraud.

The Speaker of the House had been diverting funds from the budget of the House into a personal account. The House had its bank account into which all monies received on behalf of the House were deposited and it was clearly against the rules to transfer money into a personal account. Whenever it was necessary to withdraw money for approved purposes, the signatories to the account, in this case, the Speaker, the Deputy Speaker, and Ade as *ex-officio* signatory, withdrew the money and handed it over to whoever had the responsibility of utilising the money—which in most cases was the Speaker himself.

Ade discovered, from an associate of the Speaker, that the Speaker would regularly deduct certain sums from the amounts given him for use on behalf of the House and deposit them in his own account and then announce that the money had been duly spent.

With the aid of the alarmed manager of the school branch of the bank, Ade was able to obtain bank statements that showed a parallel relationship between the House withdrawals and the Speaker's deposits. They were not conclusive evidence of fraud in a law court, but they were circumstantial enough to be extremely persuasive of villainy in a political setting.

Ade realised that a public revelation of the fraud would destabilise the Student Union and reflect on the general integrity of the House. Accordingly, he privately confronted the Speaker with his findings and told him that while he had no personal animosity against him and would be reluctant to present his discovery to the House, he could not have the Speaker continue in office. Ade demanded the Speaker's resignation within a week.

The Speaker was a reasonable character who knew when he had played a game and lost. He agreed to resign and pleaded with Ade to keep the issue between them. They shook hands and parted.

In the week of the ultimatum, several thoughts confused Ade. He knew that with this evidence he had against the Speaker, he could manipulate his way through and easily become the next Speaker. He suddenly became interested in holding the office. With that thought in mind, he also had to recheck his motivations in forcing the existing Speaker out of office, wondering if he should still insist on the

Speaker's resignation. Ade also knew that he could play a political game and bargain with the Speaker's opponents — if he could force out the Speaker, they should readily support him to become the next Speaker. Since the Speaker was already on the way out, getting the title would be a cinch.

Ade dismissed his manipulative thoughts and instead allowed events to take their natural course.

At the end of the week, the Speaker called for a special sitting of the House and then with deliberate melodrama, he announced his resignation from the office of Speaker for "personal reasons". The House was astonished. They had been caught by surprise.

Hurriedly, the Deputy Speaker called for a new election into the office of Speaker. To Ade's astonishment, the outgoing Speaker nominated him as a candidate, this nomination was seconded from several quarters, and with the strength of the ex-Speaker's political support and the general goodwill he had built over the years, Ade was elected to the office of Speaker.

Ade led the House with outward calm but inward turmoil. There were lots of issues to settle and even more decisions to make. There were moments of exhilaration at the completion of his tasks and there were days of despair. The entire university campus was now his jurisdiction and he had to make weekly visits to all faculties to ascertain the welfare of the students. He received complaints from students and acted promptly on them either personally or through the Student Union President. Consequently, he found himself constantly in the office of the Vice Chancellor to discuss pressing matters. He encouraged the Vice Chancellor to set up a monthly meeting with the student leaders where grievances could be tabled and addressed. He was also always in constant battles of words with the Student Union executives in a bid to ensure that they performed their duties in the student body.

As the months passed, Ade's name became synonymous with fairness and wisdom. He became a welcome presence wherever he went on campus. He was a legend to the first year students and they would point him out in awe to their colleagues whenever they saw him.

His own classmates, veterans of years of academic toil, had matured considerably. No longer the bickering lot of the first year, they now had a possessory attitude towards Ade. They continually challenged him for paying less attention to his own class and more attention to school affairs. Members of his class would often eagerly tell some other person an anecdote or story to validate their mostly self-professed personal acquaintance with Ade. It was "a matter of pride" for his classmates to tell other students in the school that they could dress Ade down if he behaved *nonsensically*.

Ade was generally amused by his classmates' complaints but he still always made out some time to fulfil responsibilities in his class. He was even appointed as class representative, but ironically, he had to refuse the same post he had once contested for, pleading that he now had too many responsibilities outside the class. Seun had long abandoned any semblance of authority in the class and so the fourth year class was without an official class representative. Whenever Ade's classmates insisted that Ade was the class rep, he would shrug his arms smiling, and then delegate tasks to some of his classmates.

Ade's tenure as Speaker was short. He had merely taken over to complete the previous Speaker's term and just as he was settling into the comforts of his office, elections for a new Student Union government came along as the session drew to an end.

IV. The Student Union President

When Ade announced his intention to run for the office of Student Union President in his fifth year, all prior contestants simply stood down—a situation which made Ade feel a little culpable. For the first time in the history of the University, there emerged a Student Union President who was elected unopposed. Ade was sworn into office, not in the amphitheatre: the usual venue for such events, but in the Main Auditorium of the school. It was an event that was jointly hosted by the school authorities and the students. And with good reason too.

During his short tenure as Speaker of the Student Union House of Representatives, Ade had proven that students and the school authorities could live and work in harmony. The professors and other senior staff of the university had come to know and like him. He had handled the problems brought before him with a maturity that astonished them. They had been used to the *area boy* antics of previous Student Union leaders who chanted solidarity songs and thundered platitudes in long speeches, but did nothing except cause animosity between the students and the authorities. Ade had been different; he had shown that rational dialogue could find its way to the minds, and indeed, the hearts of concerned parties.

Ade had never threatened to unleash the potent powers of a mass of angry students against the authorities. He had never called for or encouraged a protest, not because he did not believe in the use of protests, but because the issues involved were too trivial in the circumstances to warrant a protest. A protest, he often said, was the option to take when reasonable dialogue had failed. Never before dialogue.

During one of his speeches criticising a planned strike by the country's labour union, he explained his opinion in similar fashion:

"I am disappointed in this idea of a *warning strike* by the labour union. You are either on strike or you are not. If labour believes there is room for negotiation, then by all means let them negotiate. But they should not embark on a strike before making their demands and giving the demands time to be implemented. You go on strike *after* making demands and the ultimatum has lapsed. And when you do go on a protest, you have to *keep protesting* until all your demands have been met."

Whenever his colleagues became anxious about demonstrations, he would point out to them that they were not behaving like university students, but like market touts. Only few university students were comfortable with being referred to as ignorant and illiterate and so the thought of these epithets were generally sufficient to silence the agitators.

With these past exhibitions of his character traits, the students and staff of the school were jointly eager to inaugurate him as the new President of the Student Union. Ade was not just a student leader; he was being flaunted as an asset to the country. His tenure as the President of the Student Union was predicted by general consensus to be a calm one, the kind that had been widely regarded as unattainable.

Politicians generally recognise potential rivals and opponents, and in a bid to secure the loyalty of the budding leader, the governor of the state sent a congratulatory message to Ade, along with a scholarship award for all future academic pursuits. With the recognition by the state government, several organisations that had never heard of him prior to his inauguration began to pursue him to speak at events and programs.

The days became a whirl during Ade's last year in school. He was practically everywhere doing everything. Faces came and went— temporary characters without lasting impressions. Ade had little time for frivolities and more time for public service. He was already a darling of the local media whom he had constantly supplied quotes and sound bites since his days as Speaker. But now, the national media courted him for interviews. Ade was on the rise as a national figure, and his name was already on the lips of students in other universities across the country. True to his character, Ade was becoming active in the National Association of University Students, gradually taking on responsibilities that brought him in contact with national politicians.

These extra-varsity activities did not prevent Ade from performing his duties within his own university, but he had less work to do and his job was basically to maintain the structures that he had helped put in place as the Speaker of the House. He got along fine with his own cabinet members and all was generally peaceful on campus.

Nothing seemed able to stop Ade now. The future he had privately anticipated for himself was in view. The country was so bad that even a little effort could propel him to the forefront of its politics. There were a lot of opportunities for his input.

It was one late night sometime in the middle of January while still in the first semester of his final year that Ade finally came face to face with the mechanics of a country that ensured the futility of carefully laid plans.

He was returning from a lecture at the British Council, the night was fine for January, and he was driving a friend's car. His subconscious mind drove the car while he mentally scheduled his activities for the next day, part of which included a presentation of gifts to a motherless babies' home on behalf of the Student Union. He was squeamish around babies and he mused to himself about the paradox in his being able to face a bunch of student rouges and other rough characters, and yet panic when facing innocent children.

He was driving on the Third Mainland Bridge when suddenly an unusual checkpoint emerged in the glare of his headlights. He slowed down almost to a halt. The flickers of the policemen's flashing torches waving their hands bounced confusedly across his windscreen, and uncertain whether he was required to stop or to go on ahead, he momentarily pedalled on the accelerator instead of his brake, propelling the car forward.

Seeing the alarmed reactions from the policemen, he hurriedly brought the car to a complete halt just before he went past the check - point. His efforts were futile. A splattering of bullets from the excited policemen pierced the rear windscreen of the car. One of the bullets found a fatal trajectory, shot into his necksevered a carotid artery and, once and for all time, stamped a full stop to Adesand his countrysonward progression.